J. T. EDSON'S
FLOATING OUTFIT

The toughest bunch of Rebels that ever lost a war, they fought for the South, and then for Texas, as the legendary Floating Outfit of "Ole Devil" Hardin's O.D. Connected ranch.

MARK COUNTER was the best-dressed man in the West: always dressed fit-to-kill. **BELLE BOYD** was as deadly as she was beautiful, with a "Manhattan" model Colt tucked under her long skirts. **THE YSABEL KID** was Comanche fast and Texas tough. And the most famous of them all was **DUSTY FOG**, the ex-cavalryman known as the Rio Hondo Gun Wizard.

J. T. Edson has captured all the excitement and adventure of the raw frontier in this magnificent Western series. Turn the page for a complete list of Berkley Floating Outfit titles.

J. T. EDSON'S
FLOATING OUTFIT
WESTERN ADVENTURES
FROM BERKLEY

J.T. Edson

QUIET TOWN

BERKLEY BOOKS, NEW YORK

This book was first published under a
pseudonym of J. T. Edson, Chuck Nolan.

QUIET TOWN

A Berkley Book / published by arrangement with
Transworld Publishers, Ltd.

PRINTING HISTORY
Originally published in Great Britain
by Brown Watson Ltd.
Corgi edition published 1968
Berkley edition / September 1980

ISBN: 0-425-04623-0

A BERKLEY BOOK® TM 757,375
Berkley Books are published by Berkley Publishing Corporation,
200 Madison Avenue, New York, New York 10016.
PRINTED IN THE UNITED STATES OF AMERICA

CHAPTER ONE

Citizen's Arrest

Quiet Town wasn't. Fact being, since that day, eight months before, when gold was struck in the hills, the town had been far from quiet. The gold vein was still paying in the same quantities, even though there were gloomy predictions that it would not last. However, the rich vein still poured forth, and money still flowed into the capacious pockets of the business men of the town.

From a raw frontier hamlet of some twenty houses Quiet Town swelled into a square mile or more of saloons, dancehalls, gambling hells, brothels, stores and houses. It was built in a rough square, and based on a cross formed by Grant Street, flowing roughly East to West, and Lee Street running just as roughly North to South. At the flourishing crossroads stood the four largest and most imposing buildings of the town. These were Bearcat Annie's Saloon, unusual in that it was operated by a woman, the Golden Gal Dancehall, Irish Pat's

Whisky Parlour and the Beaumain Theatre on whose rough boards had appeared some of the most famous and talented performers of the day.

Working away from these four examples of civic pride the rest of the town straggled off with typical Western disregard for planning and neat arrangement. The buildings were of different standards of splendour, depending on the financial status of the owners. Amongst the largest and most prosperous of all was Buzzard Grimwood's Funeral Parlour. This was the only such business in the town and Grimwood lived in some style on the profits made by his hearses.

Not that Quiet Town had any need to be ashamed of any of her civic amenities. The jail and town marshal's office was a large and imposing stonebuilt structure which the City Fathers fondly hoped would pay for itself in imposed fines. The bank was also built of stone and its vaults often held more wealth than most Eastern banks saw in a year. The rest of the buildings were mostly built of timber, the houses of the citizens neither so large or well made as the business section.

Day and night the town boomed wide open. The miners came pouring in from the diggings with their money hanging heavily in their pockets. They wanted to be relieved of the weight and the good citizens were only too eager to help with the removing. No honest women dare to be seen after dark on the streets. The crash of shots was no strange sound and men died violently to the tune of roaring guns. They were tough and hard men who ripped their living from the Montana hills. There was just as rough a crowd waiting to relieve the miners of their wealth, none hampered by scruples and few with self-restraint. The painted girls who could and did walk the streets after dark were obliged to carry one of Henry Deringer, or his many copiers', little pistols on their person. All were willing to use it to defend, if not their honour, whatever else they held dear.

To add to this throng came Texas cowhands, bringing herds to sell to the meat-hungry miners, or visiting after trailing a herd to the Kansas railheads. They came to spend their pay and did not help to make Quiet Town any more civilized or sedate for every man of them walked armed and was willing to use his guns with little or no provocation.

It was one of these wild sons of the saddle who gave Quiet Town its name. He came into town and in the course of two hours saw a fatal shooting, a knife fight, a brawl which wrecked a saloon and an explosion caused by a drunken miner gaily tossing a stick of dynamite into a vacant lot. The Texan studied all of this then went into Bearcat Annie's place and announced:

"I'd tell a man this is one quiet town."

The cowhand's words were treated with the honour they deserved and the cowhand was feted until he left. The name came and stuck and instead of being called Gillem the metropolis became Quiet Town.

So Quiet Town was named and prospered, its sidewalks ringing to the thud of boots and the air shattered by shots. The hearses of Buzzard Grimwood were pulled by their teams of matched blacks to and from the various killings, the wheels helping to churn up and hide from sight the bloodstains on the streets.

A wise man that Grimwood. He had been one of the first citizens to arrive after the gold strike. Thinking over what he'd seen in other such towns he approached the City Fathers with a proposition. There was to be no cheap boothill in Quiet Town, every man who died here was to receive a proper burial. The City Fathers, full of civic pride, agreed. Grimwood knew many who died would be broke so he pressed for, and was granted,

payment by the town for any such as died. The City
Fathers were proud of their liberal and progressive attitude until, too late, they discovered Grimwood was fast
becoming the richest man in town. He was the only
undertaker; two more started in opposition but fell by
the wayside.

The law in Quiet Town was all but nonexistent. Three
good men held the badge and died wearing it. Now a
drunken, cowardly loafer disgraced the office of Marshal
of Quiet Town. The City Fathers, aware of what was
happening, fumed and tried to get Hickok, Dan Troop
or Matt Dillon, but all three were fully engaged by the
Kansas trailend towns and could not come. The leader
of the City Fathers, old Matt Gillem wrote to a good
friend in Texas but so far he had heard nothing from the
friend.

The poker game in Irish Pat's Whisky Parlour attracted little or no attention. For one thing it was early
Monday morning, for another, in a place where thou-
sands were won and lost, a game with a five dollar limit
was nothing to bother about. The players were a varied
group, a miner, two Texas cowhands and a professional
gambler called Baker. Of the four only Baker was known
around the town and even he was not well known. He
was a newcomer, having recently arrived from one of
the Kansas trailend towns, he and a hulking man called
Bull Moose. They went around the small stake games.
Baker playing and Moose watching. Neither were easy
in their minds and watched any cowhand who came near
with worried eyes. When new Texas men came into town
Baker and his friend would look them over from a distance before going near.

Behind the bar Irish Pat glanced at the game, then at
his only other customers, members of the Town Council.
These sat at their usual table, working out how much

damage had been done in the revels of the weekend. They were small, wizened and untidy looking Sam Gillem, the banker; Frank Barsen, who with Irish Pat represented the saloon keepers; Hans Soehnen and Angus McTavish who spoke for the mine owners and miners; Will Lealen, the gunsmith, and Bradgate from the hardware store who were the business men's representatives. They were talking and Irish Pat left the bar untended to join them.

The poker players were not so absorbed in their game that they could not spare a glance at the batwing doors as they opened to admit two men. One was tall and would have caught the eye, the other smaller, insignificant looking. They were a pair of Texas cowhands and Baker looked them over with worried eyes.

The taller of the pair was Indian dark, his face almost babyishly innocent. His black Stetson hat, low of crown and widely brimmed, was pushed back and his hair was so black it shone almost blue. His red hazel eyes were not young, and they held something which made a man think twice before he dismissed that black-dressed boy. From hat to boots the young man wore all black; even his gunbelt was of black leather. Only the walnut grips of the old Dragoon gun holstered butt forward at his right and the ivory hilt of the bowie knife at his left were not black. There was something wild and Indian about this boy, something the two Texas men could read far better than any of the others.

The other man was smaller, not more than five foot six as opposed to the six foot of his friend. He was far from the eye catching kind. His Texas style black Stetson was also pushed back, his hair a dusty blond colour. His face was tanned, handsome. To a man who could read the signs it showed power, strength and intelligence. A tight-rolled, long blue bandana was knotted around his throat and the end hung almost to the waistband of his levis. His dark blue shirt was new looking, tucked into his levis. These were cowhand style, the legs hanging outside over his expensive and fancy stitched boots, the <u>cuffs</u> turned back. Around his waist was a hand-carved buscadero gunbelt, butt forward in the holsters, a matched brace of white-handled Colt 1860 Army revolvers.

For a moment they stood at the door, looking around, then moved forward. The black dressed boy walked with a catlike grace, giving the impression that he could cross dry sticks without making a sound. At the table they halted, looking at the players and the smaller spoke:

"Room for players?"

Baker looked the two men over, licking his lips nervously. Before he could make any reply the miner grinned and waved to the empty chairs. "Sure, set and play on with us. Five dollar limit."

The small man took a seat then glanced at his friend. "You playing, Lon?"

"Nope. My pappy allus allowed a man shouldn't take likker, cards nor women on an empty stomach. I'll just take me something from the free lunch there."

While his friend walked towards the free lunch counter the small man looked over the other players in the game. The miner was big, and bearded, with the sleeves of his shirt rolled up from his brawny arms. One of the two cowhands was tall, his hat hung on the back of his chair. His hair was black, his face studious and pale, yet it was a tan resisting pallor. A gay coloured bandana was knotted at his throat and his shirt was open at the neck, the collar over the collar of his coat. The brown coat's right side was stitched back to leave clear the ivory butt of the Army Colt at his side.

The other cowhand was a couple of inches smaller,

wide shouldered and with rusty red hair. He wore Texas cowhand dress and holstered at his side was a Dance Bros. revolver. He handled his cards with a flourish and introduced the other players. "This here's," he indicated the other cowhand, "my pard, Doc Leroy. This's Mike and this's Baker. I'm Rusty Willis."

"Howdy," the small man said, taking a billfold from his shirt and extracting some money. "Call me Dusty."

Rusty Willis and Doc Leroy exchanged glances. They knew cowhands and knew that despite his small size and insignificant appearance this young man was a top-hand of his and their trade. They knew something of a man called Dusty. So did the gambler. Baker looked to where his friend, Bull Moose, lounged against the bar and made a sign. The hulking man came forward, moving around the table to halt as if to stand and kibitz with the players. He stood just behind the small Texan called Dusty.

Rusty Willis dealt the cards, flipping them out fast across the table. The others looked at their hands. Baker held a stack of silver dollars in his right hand, stacking them up and down nervously. The others sat with their attention on their cards. Dusty looked up and remarked, "I learned this game from a kinsman of mine. A man called Lane Clements."

Baker gave a muffled curse, the coins shooting from his hand to roll in front of Rusty Willis who brushed them aside. "I knows I'm going to take the hand, friend," he said. "But let's give you the pleasure of playing them first."

But despite the cheerful words there was a subtle difference in the air of the game. The miner could feel it less than the two cowhands. Baker glanced at each of the three cowhands. There did not appear to be any connection between them, Doc Leroy and Rusty Willis had been in town since Friday and this other man was newly arrived. Baker was sure they were strangers, but he was wary now and, looming behind the small Texan, Bull Moose was scowling.

The hand finished with Rusty taking the pot and the cards passing to Baker. The man scowled as he riffed the cards leaving five hearts on the bottom of the deck. He held the cards out for the miner to cut and Mike did as he had been doing all the time, just tapped the deck without cutting. Then Baker took the cards in his left hand, three fingers gripping the long edge, the index finger curling around the short edge as if to hold the deck square.

Dusty was watching everything. He saw a glint in Doc Leroy's eyes and spoke, his voice still that soft, even drawl yet somehow full of menace. "Turn your cards, gambling man. If you've got five hearts—!"

Baker flung back his chair, hand going under his coat to the butt of his singleshot Derringer. At the same moment Bull Moose dropped his shoulder and tried to knock the Texan from his feet as he rose. Only Dusty did not rise. It was as if he knew what was going to happen for instead of coming to his feet as had the others he fell sideways from his chair. Baker saw the move but was too late to correct his aim. The Derringer roared out, throwing its deadly load full into Bull Moose's body. Dusty landed, his left hand holding a Colt even before he hit the floor. His right hand fanned the hammer fast, three shots came in a single roll of sound. The table top erupted in splinters and Baker rocked backwards, going down as dead as a man could be when hit under the chin with three .44 bullets which came out through the top of his head.

Dusty came to his feet, his gun smoking in his hand. He twisted to look at the members of the town council who were all on their feet at the table. Then he stepped

forward to kick the Derringer away from Baker's hand.
He bent and looked at the man, then straightened again
and went to look at Bull Moose who was on his back
and gasping his last.

Doc Leroy stepped forward and turned Baker's cards
over, five hearts were exposed to view. "You got real
quick eyes friend, and quicker hands. I saw him use the
grip and fetch them from the bottom. Was all set to call
him myself."

"Man'd say you knew how he aimed to make his
play," Rusty went on.

"That was how they downed my cousin, Lane Clements down to Newton. Dan Troop told me about it."

Rusty Willis and Doc Leroy showed no surprise at
the statement. They knew the deep loyalty to the clan
all southern men felt. Naturally this young man called
Dusty would seek out and have a reckoning with any
man who killed his kinsman like that. What surprised
them was that Dan Troop would give any information
about a killing to some chance passing stranger. It told
them even more about that soft talking, insignificant
man.

"Say one thing, the big *hombre* had sand to burn,"
Rusty remarked, looking down at Bull Moose. "Standing
right behind you while his pard shot."

"There's not too much risk. A Derringer won't throw
a ball clear through a man," Dusty answered. "He
was—."

The saloon door was thrown open and the men
crowded in. All but one of them were town dressed,
fresh faced dudes with the stamp of new arrivals in the
West. The other man was a bleary eyed, dirty and untidy
looking individual in rumpled clothes and with the badge
of town marshal tarnished upon his shirt. In his right
hand he held a rusted Beals Navy revolver which he

pointed halfheartedly at the group who stood by the table.

"Who done it?" he asked while his escort hefted the shotguns they held.

"I did," the small Texan replied.

Looking at the marshal, guns in leather, the small man waited. "You're under arrest, then."

"What charge?"

The marshal licked his lips and did not speak. A fair haired, handsome young man standing just behind the marshal answered, "For murder."

"That's a hard word, friend," Lon said, moving from the bar to flank his friend. "Let's go find—."

The marshal studied the tall, Indian dark boy as he stood alongside his friend. There was something latently dangerous about him. The lawman thrust his Beals forward in what he hoped was a threatening manner but which more resembled a schoolboy holding out his hand for the teacher to cane. His voice was cracked as he said, "I got a gun in my hand."

"Drop it!"

The voice came from behind the men, at the door they had just entered. It was a deep, southern drawl, a voice with authority. The voice of a man who stood behind a cocked and lined gun.

Dropping his gun as if it was redhot the Marshal looked at the bar mirror to see who this newcomer was. Anger flooded to his whiskery and dirty face as he saw the reflection. The batwing doors were pushed open and leaning his shoulder against the jamb was as fine a look-ing specimen of manhood the marshal had ever seen. Full three inches over six foot he stood. On his head a costly lowcrowned white Stetson with a silver concha decorated band. His hair was a rich, golden blond, his face almost classically handsome. Around his neck was a tight rolled, long red silk bandana, flowing down over the expensive tan shirt which was tailored to the great spread of his shoulders and slender waist. A wide, brown leather gunbelt was around his waist, in the low tied holsters a matched brace of ivory handled Colt Army revolvers. His hands held nothing more dangerous than a half smoked cigarette.

In sudden fury the marshal bent to grab up the Beals again, but the handsome blond giant moved forward to stand on the other flank of the man called Dusty.

"Leave her lie, *hombre*," the newcomer ordered. "You don't need her one lil bit."

He moved forward slightly and kicked the gun to one side with a contemptuous foot, then fell back again to flank his friends once more. The marshal never made a move either to stop or interfere with the big cowhand.

It was the young dude who'd spoke up who made the next move, trying to prod the marshal into action. "Do your duty, marshal."

The marshal gulped, looking at those three tanned and efficient men who stood before him. Unlike his backing party he knew the West and knew cowhands. Those three were as handy as men could be. His hand went up to rub his face as he gasped out, "I don't feel any too good."

The words were greeted by an angry rumble from the men at his back and their spokesman snapped, "You never do when there's trouble. That's why we're living in this sort of town. We've got to stop these killers."

"Then you stop them, Mr. Bigmouth Kennet," the marshal replied as he removed his badge and hurled it on the floor. "I'm not getting killed. *You* take them!"

Kennet watched the marshal blunder past him, then glanced at the other fresh faced dudes. He turned and squared his shoulders back though he still did not lift his shotgun from under his arm. "All right. I'm making a citizen's arrest. I'm taking you in on a charge of murder."

"Hey, Doc!" Rusty Willis spoke up, taking everything in. "We ain't going to stand here and watch them fierce ole Yankees abusing these poor defenceless lil ole Texas boys, now are we?"

"Ole Stone'd be right mortified with us if we did and the rest of the boys wouldn't talk to us for a month," Doc replied. "So with Cap'n Fog's permission I reckon we'll sit in with him."

"Cap'n Fog?" Irish Pat and the rest of the Town Council were watching and listening. It was the Irishman who spoke. "Holy mother of god, Matt. You've got to stop this or your banker boy'll get hisself and his friends killed. I know who they are now. The tall blond boy's Mark Counter, the dark one the Ysabel Kid."

"Then you mean that small man's Dusty Fog?" McTavish asked.

CHAPTER TWO

The Man Gillem Sent For

The group of twelve townsmen, their shot guns held under their arms, faced the five young Texans, not knowing who or what kind of men they were matched against. If they had known they might have thought twice before attempting their folly.

Dusty Fog, the small insignificant looking young man, was already a legend in his own lifetime. In the War between the States he had been a Cavalry Captain at seventeen and as a raider built a name equalled only by the old Dixie masters, Mosby and Turner Ashby. Dusty Fog was the man who after the War went into Mexico to bring back General Bushrod Sheldon in face of Maximillian's French army.* Since then Dusty was fast carving himself a name in the annals of border gunplay and as a cowhand par-excellence. He was no man for a bunch of shotgun armed dudes to fool with or try to arrest.

*Told in THE YSABEL KID

Mark Counter was also a name in his own right. His skill with any or all branches of cattlework was as high if not higher than Dusty's. In the war he had been the Beau Brummel of Sheldon's army, his sartorial taste much copied. Now he was a cow country fashion plate and cowhands from the Rio Grande to the Indian Nations copied Mark Counter's dress style. Yet there was more than a dandy to Mark. He was a fist fighter of note with the strength of a giant combined with speed. His ability with his gun was not so well known even though reliable witnesses of such things ranked him among the five fastest men in Texas.

The Ysabel Kid was also a legend in his own lifetime and an exciting, eventful lifetime it had been. Down on the Rio Grande there would have been no such folly as this arrest attempt tried, for they knew the way of the Ysabel Kid down there. He was the product of a union between a wild Irish-Kentuckian fighting man and a French Creole-Comanche woman, each of the bloods giving some talent. From his father he got a love of fighting coupled with caution and wisdom while fighting. It gave him also the sighting eye of an eagle and an ability to handle his Winchester rifle with the skill of the legendary backwoodsmen. From his mother's side the Comanche strain showed in his wolf-keen nerves and senses, in his ability to ride anything with hair. From the French Creole he got a love of cold steel as a fighting weapon and the inborn prowess with his Bowie knife that would not have shamed the men who designed the knife. Add to that a knowledge of six Indian languages, the ability to follow a track where a buck Apache would be beaten, the ability to move as silently as a ghost. That was the Ysabel Kid. These dudes with their shotguns held awkwardly were going to try the Ysabel Kid and his friends, put them under arrest.

Even the other men were out of place in this company. Rusty Willis and Doc Leroy worked as trail hands for Stone Hart's Wedge, an outfit of contract drivers. The Wedge took cattle north from Texas to whatever market they could find, handling cattle for the small ranchers who could not afford to make up their own herds. It was Stone Hart's Wedge which smashed the stranglehold of Jethro Kliddoe, an ex-Union Army officer who was stopping the trail drives and taking head tax on the cattle. To work for the Wedge a man needed to be a top hand with cattle, and he was also likely to be good with a gun.

These then were the five men the dudes, full of their Eastern ideals, were going to match against with shotguns. They did not know that the Ysabel Kid, who did not account himself fast with a gun, could draw and shoot in about one second. At least two of the men facing the dudes could draw and shoot in half that time and guarantee putting a .44 ball where it would do most good at the end of the half second.

Kennet glanced back at his friends again, making what could have been a fatal mistake. In the time Kennet was looking away, Dusty and his friends could have laid at least half of them dead on the floor. Kennet and his friends were all well educated, fresh out of Eastern colleges and full of theories on life, conduct and morals. They were banded together here in an attempt to clean up Quiet Town as they had banded together back East in their colleges when they believed something needed altering. By prodding the marshal they had hoped to make a start at cleaning up the town; now they had no marshal and were led by a man who had no conception of just how fast and deadly a topgun like Dusty Fog or Mark Counter was. They were in far more danger than they had ever faced.

"Look friend," the miner spoke up; *he* knew the danger all too well. "You got this all wrong. There was nothing unfair in the shooting."

"We'd expect you to say that," Kennet replied. "You were in the game."

Dusty was getting tired of the dudes' foolishness. He knew he could rely on Mark and the Kid not to do anything rash or foolish. He was almost sure Rusty and Doc were also reliable and would not go off halfcocked. All too well Dusty knew the danger of the situation. If shooting started he would down at least two of the men before they could even think of killing, the other Texans would also be in action before the dudes knew what they were doing.

"Look, if you want to hold a coroner's jury we'll all come and testify," he suggested, giving the dudes a chance to get out without loss of face.

Kennet shook his head. "We intend to try you for murder."

Dusty shrugged. He had offered the olive branch and the dudes refused it. Now it was on their heads for he would never give up his guns to any man. The dudes must stand or fall on their own decision.

"You'll have to take him first," Mark warned.

"Hold hard there, all of you!" Mat Gillem was on his feet and crossing the room. "Stan boy, you stop this foolishness afore you get yourself and your friends killed off."

Kennet turned to Gillem, surprise showing on his face. Since coming to act as manager of Gillem's bank he had grown used to the old man's good sense and to respect his judgment. Gillem's attitude came as a surprise to him for the banker wanted Quiet Town cleaned up too.

"We have to make a stand, sir," he objected. "These

killings can't be allowed to go unpunished."

"Son, there was nothing wrong in Cap'n Fog killing that gambler. Baker was cheating and tried to gun Dusty after Moose made a try at knocking Dusty off balance. You go ahead with this citizen's arrest foolishness and they'll be burying at least half of you. There was no murder. Baker died of a case of slow."

All too often Kennet had heard that expressive range term. A case of slow. It meant exactly what it said. One of the participants in a corpse-and-cartridge affair was not as fast as the other and paid the penalty for lack of speed.

The other men with Kennet looked at each other. It was suddenly dawning on them that here it was different from the pampered East with its police to protect them from the consequences of their actions. Back East they had often campaigned against things, and with the fervour of the college students they had so recently been they started to campaign in Quiet Town. One thing they forgot was that although they had been allowed to campaign, in the West a man could do pretty well as he pleased, they could only rely on themselves to carry their campaigns through. In the West a man who wanted to change things was at liberty to do so, just as long as he could back up his play with a fast handled Colt.

"There is nothing to stop them coming in for a trial then," Kennet answered. He was still not sure what to make of Gillem's attitude in squashing this try at taming Quiet Town.

"Son, this ain't the East. If you try to take Captain Fog and he wants he can down four of you before you even get your scatters off your arms. The other boys are near as fast and good. You let it drop."

Dusty and the other Texans relaxed now. They could guess there would be no more trouble. The old timer appeared to have things well in hand, and was holding the dudes in check.

"We can't go on allowing every man who wears a gun to scare us," Kennet objected. "Or we'll—."

"Son, these aren't just any men. You start to lift your shotgun off your arm ready to shoot and see."

Kennet started to swing his shotgun from his arm, then he froze. The Ysabel Kid twisted the palm of his hand out, bringing the old Dragoon from leather and lining it cocked ready. "Mister," his voice sardonic as he lowered the hammer between the safety notches of the cylinder and holstered the gun again, "I'm the slowest of us five."

With that he turned and followed his friends to the bar where the bardog who'd arrived greeted them with a grin.

"Like I say," Gillem looked at the scared faces. "They aren't just any men. And don't think the Ysabel Kid was joshing you. He *is* the slowest of them."

The batwing doors swung open to let a tall, thin, cadaverous man enter. On his head was a black high hat with a black crepe band around it. His thin face looked like it was mummified and held an expression of mournful piety. His white shirt and sober black tie, his Prince Albert coat, trousers and shoes all looked expensive. His face never changed expression as he crossed the room and looked down at the two bodies. Bending over he pulled Baker's wallet out and looked inside.

"Two of them," his voice was harsh and cracked. "When will it all end?"

"There was enough to pay for the burying of both of them?" Gillem was practical.

"This one can pay his way, the other is broke and will be charged to the town."

"You're a cold blooded swine, Grimwood," Kennet

snapped, not hiding his dislike for the other man. "You earn the name of Buzzard."

The sallow face never changed expression and the voice showed no feeling yet there was a hard glint in the black eyes. "It is well I abhor violence, young man, or I could take offence at that remark."

"You abhor violence, but you rob the dead in the streets," Kennet snorted.

Grimwood ignored the young man as if he was not there. He went to the door and called in his assistants, told them to remove the bodies and went out. Kennet watched him go with disgust plain on his face, then turned to sit at the table with the Town Council.

At the bar Dusty watched the departure of the undertaker, then turned to the others. "If I die here don't you let him get his cotton-picking claws on me."

"You're safe," Mark answered. "Only the good die young."

"Sure," Rusty Willis agreed. "It surely surprises me that I've lasted this long. Say, I'm Rusty Willis and this's Doc Leroy. We ride for the—."

"Wedge," Dusty finished for him. "We came into Abilene with a herd from the OD Connected a couple of months after you boys rode over Kliddoe."

"Yeah." The Kid's voice was soft but there was a hard look on his face and a Comanche meanness in his eyes. "It was a pity. I wanted to see old Yellerdawg real bad."

"Friend of your'n?" Doc inquired, knowing no deep south boy would willingly go out of his way to see a man like Kliddoe.

"Not yet. I got me a present for him when we do meet."*

*How the Kid delivered it is told in TRAIL BOSS

Before any of the others could make comment on this remarkable statement the bardog interrupted, pointing to the City Fathers at their table. "The gents want to have a word with you, Cap'n Fog."

Dusty walked away and Mark gave his attention to Doc and Rusty. "Say, are all the stories I've heard about Peaceful Gunn true?"

Rusty and Doc grinned; their friend and fellow driver Peaceful Gunn was something of a character. "If they don't cover cowardice, letting down his *amigos* and all other nefarious practices," Doc replied.

"What's these here nef—nerfar—whatever you said?" the Kid inquired.

"Don't you pay ole Doc no never mind, Kid," Rusty warned. "He got that way when our cook fed him on letter biscuits."

Dusty went to the table and Gillem came to his feet holding out his hand in a warm greeting. "Howdy, Cap'n Fog. See Ole Devil got my letter. Gents, this here's the man I sent for."

Dusty looked puzzled. "I don't follow you. I brought a herd north for Uncle Devil. What letter are you talking about?"

"Ole Devil didn't send you here then?" There was a disappointment in Gillem's voice.

"Nope. The gambler killed one of my kin in Newton. Cut a rusty on him. Dan Troop told me what happened and I trailed him up here. Did you write to Uncle Devil for help?"

"Yeah. Thought that was why you'd come. We need us some law in this town."

"I don't see how I can help. Could recommend Hickok, Matt Dillon or maybe Dan Troop. His contract with Newton expires at the end of the month and I reckon he wouldn't object to a change of scenery."

"It's only the second of the month now, Cap'n Fog. I'll write for Troop to come along but we still have all this month and no law. We reckon you're just what we want."

Dusty looked around the table, his eyes flinty and hard. "I don't sell my guns, mister."

"Dangnab it to hell, boy, none of us reckon you do," Gillem answered. "We need law here and the man who takes the badge'll have to be more than just a fast gun. If all we wanted was a fast gun there's a dozen in town we could take. Sure you're fast with a gun, so's Hickok, Troop or Dillon. A lawman needs to be fast. Your pappy's no slouch either. We saw how you can handle a gun just now. We saw you could hold back from handling it, too. Hickok would have cut Stan here down without thinking twice about it. You didn't, that makes me sure you're the man we want."

Looking mollified at the apology Dusty went on, "I'm no lawman. I've helped pappy out as a deputy, sure, but I'm a cowhand, not a john law."

"You handled that business in Mexico real well," Barsen put in, "and it wasn't a cattle chore either."

"That was different. It wasn't handling the law in a boomtown like this."

"It'd take a man with the heart of a lion to tame this town down, Captain darlin'," Irish Pat's rich brogue cut in. "He'll have to handle as rough a crowd as ever took gold from the ground. It'll take a man like you."

"We've got to clean the town up, Captain Fog," Bradgate went on. "The gold strike brought in a whole lot of bad characters and the town's wide open. Look out of any window and what do you see? Saloons, dance-halls, gaming houses, brothels. Some of them are honest but many aren't. We don't want to improve our morals, most all of us have used those places in our lives and look to use them again. But we want a standard kept. There's too much crime here, too many killings, fights. We want it stopped."

"Aye laddie," McTavish's deep Scottish burr joined in. "That we do. The miners want protecting. It's getting so bad that we hardly dare let the men come in with money in their pockets for fear they'll wind up laying in an alley with a stove-in head and pockets emptied out."

"We need law here, not that dirty, cowardly sheep who you saw either." Gillem finished for the others. "How about it?"

A tall man came into the saloon before Dusty could answer, walking across the room arrogantly and halting at the table to look around with disdainful gaze. He pushed back his white Stetson, his handsome face mocking. From his frilly shirt, black cutaway jacket and tight legged grey trousers he could be told as a frontier gambler. The shining gunbelt with the lowtied, silver decorated Navy Colt was supposed to indicate he was a good man with a gun also.

"Heard you were meeting," he said, glancing at Dusty. "Why wasn't I called?"

"Why should you be?" Gillem growled, looking back. "You were never voted on to the council."

The gambler's hand fell to his side, caressing the butt of his gun. "I've got six votes here for me. Likewise I'm saying we aren't having any Texas gunwolf running the law here."

Dusty's cigarette flipped from his fingers, the end hitting the gambler's shirt and leaving a black mark. "Mister, I've got twelve votes to your six which swings the election my way. Mr. Gillem, you've got yourself a Town Marshal. Are you making anything of it, gambling man?"

Their eyes met and locked, the small Texan's meeting

the gambler's with no sign of flinching. Silence fell on the room yet suddenly Gillem and the rest were not aware that Dusty was small. Suddenly he had become the biggest man in that room and seemed to tower over them all.

Then the gambler looked away, unable to meet Dusty's eyes any longer. He knew who this small man was and did not intend to try and make something of it. "All right. Just remember, lawmen die fast in Quiet Town."

"Gambler's die fast any place," Dusty's voice was soft and even. "Get your hand off the gun."

The gambler knew he would never be in a better position to take Dusty than right then. His hand was on his gunbutt, he was that much ahead of Dusty. Yet still he was not sure. All too well he knew his own speed but the soft talking, small man was too much for him. His hand came clear of his gun butt and he turned to walk from the room again.

Matt Gillem wiped the sweat from his face. "I never thought to see Clint Fang back down that way."

"Who is he?" Dusty asked.

"Bearcat Annie's boss dealer and triggerman. He's bad medicine."

Kennet was looking at Dusty with admiration. "I see I made a mistake, Captain Fog. You'll make a very good marshal for Quiet Town."

"My friends call me Dusty. Now, I'm going to need me four deputies."

"Four deputies?" yelped McTavish, a true Scot, thinking of how much it would cost the town. "That's a lot of law."

"This's a lot of town. Five of us at the usual rates won't bankrupt you and I don't take on without good men at my back."

"Four deputies, huh?" Gillem glanced at the group

at the bar. "I know, Mark Counter and the Ysabel Kid, expected you to want them. The other two look just like ordinary cowhands to me."

"So are Mark, Lon and me. You're taking us for all of that."

"It's still a lot of law, laddie," McTavish said.

Gillem interrupted. "Okay, we'll pay you one hundred, the deputies eighty a month and you get twenty per cent of all fines—."

"No. We'll take one hundred and twenty-five for me, hundred each for the deputies and we want nothing from the fines."

"You'll be losing money on it," Gillem warned.

"Likely. But I've seen lawmen working for a share of the fines. They'd take in any man they saw on any charge, just to get money."

"All right, we take your terms. All in favour?"

The meeting was all in favour, even more so since Dusty's words on the subject of fines. Dusty took the Marshal's badge which Kennet had picked up from the floor. Then the young Texan looked around the table. "All right, gents. You've hired me until Dan Troop can get up here at the end of the month, or until you hire another suitable man. I handle the law here in town and I don't account to anyone for any action I think is necessary. I'll tread on any toes I have to."

"I've got no corns on me feet, Captain darlin'," Irish Pat boomed. "So you tread where you will."

"You'll back me on everything?" There was a twinkle in Dusty's eyes.

"Everything and more!" Irish Pat's hand smashed down on to the tabletop.

"Moonshining's illegal. How about that still you've got out back there?"

Irish Pat's face turned red and he gulped out. "Captain

darlin', you wouldn't be after taking something that's dearer to me than me mother."

Dusty laughed. He turned and walked back to join his friends at the bar. He could see they were all eager to hear why the town council wished to speak with him and did not keep them waiting. "All right, Lon, Mark, you're now deputies of the Quiet Town police force." Turning he looked at the other two cowhands. "My pappy always allows that to catch a crook you need a crook. So I reckon I'll take you two on for a spell if you like."

Doc and Rusty grinned delightedly at each other. They had come to Quiet Town ahead of the rest of the Wedge crew and were not expecting their friends for a week or so. Already they were getting bored with inactivity and this dangerous task they were being offered looked like shaping up to be good fun. They wanted to see what the other members of the Wedge said when they arrived and found them wearing law badges.

"You just hired two men," Doc said delightedly.

Dusty turned and his friends followed him back across the room to halt at the table. "All right, gents, we're on."

"There's one thing, Captain," Soehen spoke up. "The miners, especially the little men, have been having some trouble. A gang's been hitting at the gold shipments. We've tried to get a line on them but we can't. Thought it might have been some of the old Henry Plummer bunch at first. Then that it was one of the Missouri gangs. Then we heard it was Bronco Calhoun. But it can't be. The gang's got both Northern and Southern men in it."

"Unless it's two separate gangs," McTavish put in.

"No. it's a mixed gang, has been when they've hit."

"Should say that'd be more for the county sheriff to handle," Dusty remarked.

"Would be if you could tell us what county you're

in. The country's never been surveyed properly," Gillem explained. "Neither county wants to take on a town like this even if it would boost their taxes."

"All right, I'll handle it if I can," Dusty promised. "How do you move your gold out of the hills?"

"Wagons, there used to be four or five companies, operating hereabouts. Now there ain't but the one. Ole Joe Delue and his daughter Roxie. The others gave up after they had started to lose teams and men. Old Joe don't neither scare nor give up that easy."

"Where at's the jail?" Dusty inquired as Gillem stopped speaking.

"Out of here and along Lee Street. You'll find the badges for your deputies in the same, it don't lock none. Civic pound's at the back, or you can take your hosses to the livery barn. Town pays for food, their'n and your'n. Town pays for all the powder and shot you use while you work for us too."

"One thing," McTavish spoke up. "Powder and lead comes awful expensive, so buffalo 'em with your gun barrels if you can."

"I'll trade my old Dragoon gun in for a club was you to ask me nice," the Kid remarked.

"With a Dragoon why bother to waste good money on buying a club, laddie?" McTavish replied. "All you sassenachs are the same, no idea of the value of money.

CHAPTER THREE

Trouble At Bearcat Annie's

Dusty led his friends out of Irish Pat's Whisky Parlour, across the square and by the front of Bearcat Annie's large saloon. This was a large establishment, two stories high and with a veranda running all the way round it. At the downstairs windows were several people watching the young Texans with interest. Clint Fang was one of the watchers, his employer standing by his side as he pointed out the reason, or tried to, why he had not taken the small Texan on.

"Mark, you and Rusty go along and bring the hosses from the livery barn," Dusty ordered. "Then I'll read you the scriptures and swear you in."

The two parties went their separate ways. Dusty looked at the town jail and Marshal's office with satisfaction. It was a single storey stone building and looked strong enough. The front of the building was given over to the office and had a double door which opened on to

the street. There were two large, barred windows to let
light into the office. The office itself was sparsely fur-
nished, a desk in the centre, a table against one wall,
a safe with the door open in a corner, a stove at the other
side and a few chairs. Fastened to the rear wall, near the
door which led into the cells at the rear was a rack with
three Henry rifles and four shotguns in it. The desk was
dusty and the Marshal's logbook closed. Dusty opened
it to find there were no entries since the recently-retired
marshal took over. He looked around in distaste then
opened the desk drawer. Three held empty whisky bottles, the fourth the keys to the cells. Taking these he
went through the rear door and in a passage beyond was
faced with four strongly built cells and a door. Opening
the door he found a room with half-a-dozen beds in it.
There were just the beds and mattresses but that did not
worry him, for they all carried their bedrolls on their
saddles.

He tested each bed and located the softest mattress
then went back into the office to find he had a visitor.
The man sat at the desk with his feet up on its scratched
top. He wore the dress of a professional gambler and his
face was mocking as he drew on his cigar. The Ysabel
Kid and Doc Leroy lounged by the wall watching the
man with eyes which showed amusement and curiosity.

Dusty walked forward, his hand coming round to
knock the man's feet from the desk top. The gambler
looked up, an angry glint in his eyes. "Huh, so you're
the new marshal——"

"On your feet!" Dusty's voice brooked no arguments.

"I ain't——" the man began, but he did not get a
chance to finish.

Dusty lunged forward, his hands bunching the man's
lapels up as he hauled him bodily from the chair. The
gambler gave a startled grunt at the unexpected strength

and started to strain back. That was what Dusty wanted. He shoved suddenly instead of pulling and the man crashed to the floor. Snarling a curse he tried to get his gun out from under his arm.

"Go ahead!" Dusty's invitation was backed by the clicking as he eased back the hammer of his gun as it came into his right hand.

The man lay still, looking up into the yawning bore of the gun where no gun had been half a second before. He waited for the bullet to crash into him for he knew there were many lawmen who would not hesitate. "Don't shoot," he croaked. "I give it up."

"Stand up!" Dusty ordered and the man rose fast. "Lon, take his gun. Then put him to work cleaning this place up."

The gambler gulped but did not argue as the dangerous looking young Texan disarmed him. He had come with the express intention of showing Clint Fang how to handle the Texans but his intentions were changed rapidly. Leaving his prisoner working under the able care of the Ysabel Kid, Dusty returned to the living quarters and opened the door. Mark and Rusty were bringing up the horses and off saddling them at the corral of the civic pound. They hung the saddles on the corral rails for their owners to collect and put on the burros, the inverted V-shaped stands in the leanto at the rear of the jail. Out beyond the corral was Jenny's brothel, a large red lamp swinging before the door. Beyond that the rest of the red light area extended until it joined Chinese Street where the homes of the Oriental mine-workers were crowded together. That was the area they would expect most trouble from, for it was the roughest part of town.

The jail itself was situated handily, only the gunsmith's shop separating it from Bearcat Annie's saloon and the town centre. Dusty waited for Rusty and Mark to join him and went back to find the gambler working hard, dusting the desk before he swept up the jail floor.

"Take him into the cells," Dusty ordered.

Rusty and Mark escorted the gambler to the cells, the young Wedge rider grinning in delight. "I've never done this afore," he said delightedly as he locked the gambler in.

Returning to the office they found Dusty handing out the deputy badges and pinned their own on. With hands raised they took the oath of office then were informed they were members of the Quiet Town police force and such places as Jenny's were now out of bounds to them. Dusty took his seat behind the desk and looked at the others.

"Rusty, you and Doc haven't held down a law badge I reckon. There's a few small things you'd best learn and learn real fast. For the first week or so you'll work with either me or Mark all the time. Now, these are the scriptures. First, never try to arrest a man unless you're all set to draw and shoot, he might be wanted and on the run. If you go for a drunk watch him, he'll come at you until his eyes focus best, then he'll stop. You move in closer and you'll throw him right off balance. If you arrest a man make him face a wall and lean against it with both hands on it. Then if he tries to move while you're searching him kick his feet from under him. Don't ever take your eyes off a man until you've searched him and don't, no matter how friendly or harmless he looks, ever let him go out of your sight at all. Don't let him reach his hand out of sight for a smoke or anything. If you're going to a suspect in a buggy do it from behind, that way he can't run you down. While you work for me you never abuse or mishandle a prisoner. If you go into court as a witness stick only to what you know for certain, tell the truth and don't try either to help or fix

the man. If there's something you don't know tell the
Judge so. If you have to use your gun shoot to kill and
keep on shooting as long as the other man's on his feet
or still holds his gun. As long as he's still got the gun
in his hand he's dangerous, shoot him again."

Doc and Rusty looked at each other. Dusty Fog was
far different now than he had been at the saloon. There
he had been an amiable, friendly young cowhand. Here
at the jail he was a hard lawman, speaking with authority.
They stored his words up, each one knowing they would
need all the help they could get if they were to be of any
use to Dusty. Both were good with their guns yet they
knew there was more to being a lawman than just being
good with a gun.

"All right," Dusty let his words sink in then went on.
"Mark, you, Rusty and Doc clean those guns after we've
held a choosing match for the beds and got our gear
stowed. Lon, you're jailer for now, see the prisoner does
the rest of the cleaning."

"What charge you holding him on?" Mark inquired.

"Disturbing the peace should hold him," Dusty answered. "I'll fill in the jail log. Doc, Rusty, when you
go to feed or collect a prisoner you go in twos. The man
who goes into the cell gives the other his gun. Make any
other prisoners back up away from you right back to the
far end of the cell."

The gambler started to rattle on the cell bars with a
tin cup and yell out. The Ysabel Kid opened the door
and looked across the passage at the man. "Please, we'ns
are playing poker and I can't concentrate."

"You lemmee out of here!" the gambler yelled back.
"You can't do this to me!"

"I got news for you," the Kid replied, going to open
the cell door. "We just now went and done it."

The man came out of his cell and into the office.

Mark jerked his thumb to the desk and the broom. "Get to it."

The gambler opened his mouth to object then shut it again. He knew that he had made a mad mistake in thinking these young looking Texans were easy meat. So he cleaned the office out and then was pushed back into his cell with a cheerful warning he would be appearing before the Judge on the following morning.

Doc Leroy sat at the table on the side of the room cleaning a shotgun. He watched the assured way Dusty, Mark and the Kid handled themselves. They knew this business as well as they knew cattlework.

The door of the jail burst open and a man came in. "Marshal!" the man gasped to Dusty. "There's trouble down at Bearcat Annie's. Cy Bollinger, the black-smith's, causing a riot."

Dusty took up his hat and put it on. "Doc, Mark, let's go."

The three young men went out of the door with the bringer of the news coming after them. He was a thin, narrow-faced man in town clothes and seemed talkative as he walked with them. "That Bollinger," he said. "He's a mean one. You don't want to take any chances with him, Marshal."

Dusty did not reply. He could hear the noise from the saloon and saw a fair sized crowd gathering. He knew that this first task would either make his name or break it. How he handled the matter would be related through the town and he could get support from the citizens or lose it.

Pushing open the batwings Dusty went into Bearcat Annie's saloon, followed by Mark and Doc. The bar room was large, the bar long, polished and shiny ma-hogany. Behind the bar was a long mirror and shelves covered with bottles. Along one wall was a verandah and a line of stairs ran down in the centre of the room. Dusty saw all this in one quick glance, the tables and chairs of the room, the bandstand with its piano and seats for the rest of the orchestra did not interest him. Nor did the crowd who were on their feet and watching what was going on in the centre of the room. A huge man with great bulging arm muscles writhing, held another big man over his head. The big man was a black haired, wild eyed figure, on the rampage. Two other men were down, showing signs of meeting up with the fists of Cy Bollinger.

"Stop him, marshal," a man yelled.

Dusty ignored the man. He could see Doc watching him and knew that the slim young cowhand was wondering how he meant to handle this. Bollinger was not armed but he looked strong as a buffalo bull. Wild Bill Hickok's way of handling the matter would have been simple. A .44 bullet in the blacksmith's head. Doc was wondering if Dusty would use the same system.

"Bollinger!" Dusty roared. "Drop him."

The big blacksmith turned, still holding the man over his head. His rage-filled face changed, amazement taking its place. He released the man, allowing him to crash down unheeded. The shambling blacksmith snapped into an almost military brace with his hand lifting in a salute. "Howdy Cap'n Fog, sir."

Dusty did not reply to this friendly greeting, his face the hard mask of a martinet officer. He walked forward, eyes on Bollinger, lips in a tight line. "All right, Bollinger. You know where the jail is. Get down there."

The crowd drew in its collective breath. Every one present knew Bollinger to be for the most part a cheerful and amiable man. When he was roused he was terrible in his anger and no man to take orders. They waited to see him tear this small man to pieces.

"Sure Cap'n, sure!" Bollinger stepped over the fallen man and walked past him headed for the door.

A woman came down the stairs from the verandah. A tall, blonde woman who would catch the eye in any company. It did not take a man much time or intelligence to figure this was Bearcat Annie herself. Her blonde hair was piled on top of her head, two large diamonds glittering in her earlobes. Her face was beautiful in a hard way. Her green satin dress was clinging to her body. The dress was slit to the waist at the left. Her legs, clad in black silk stockings showed, rippling with muscles and graced with red garters that looked large enough to rope a longhorn steer. Her arms were bare, round and firm yet the biceps looked hard and strong.

Sweeping across the room she halted and looked at Dusty, then at Mark and Doc. "I heard you were young. You look even younger than I expected."

"Been troubled by it since I was born, ma'am," Dusty replied. "Likely I'll grow out of it in time."

She looked him over again, her full lips parting in a smile. "You handled Cy Bollinger real well."

"Sure, ma'am, didn't you think I could?" Dusty watched her face but could read little from it. "What started it?"

A man spoke up, pointing to a gambler who stood nearby. "He started to rile old Cy. Then said the Texas Light Cavalry was a no-good bunch of goldbricks."

"Did, huh?" Dusty's tones were mild.

He came round in a fast turn, his right fist swinging up to smash under the man's jaw. The gambler's head snapped back and he went clean over a table. Even as he landed a big bouncer lunged forward, hands reaching for Dusty. The small Texan's hands shot out, caught the man's wrist and jerked. The bouncer howled as his hand was twisted up behind his back. Dusty still held the wrist and moved his feet back, lifting the right to place it against the bouncer's rump. Pushing hard Dusty sent the man staggering forward and at the same time barked out, "Mark!"

Mark stepped forward, his left fist coming up to crash under the jaw of the onrushing man. The bouncer straightened up, his arms flailing wildly as he went over on to his back. Mark grinned at Dusty and blew on his knuckles.

Across the room one of the other saloon men dropped his hand towards his gun. Doc Leroy's hand made a white flutter and the ivory handled Army Colt came out of leather, hammer eared back. The man froze, his gun still undrawn and Bearcat Annie gave a shake of her head. The man's hand dropped to his side and he stood fast, his original aim forgotten. Even if his boss had not ordered him to let it drop he did not intend trying conclusions with a man as fast as that pallid, studious cowhand.

"Old Cy doesn't take to people calling down the Texas Light, ma'am," Dusty said. "He rode in it through the war. So did I."

"Bannock there never could learn to keep his mouth shut," Bearcat Annie replied. "He should have known better than try it with Cy Bollinger. He might not have known about Cy being in the Texas Light though."

Dusty held down his smile, that was like saying a man did not know Washington was the capital city of the United States. Bollinger was very proud of having served in the Texas Light Cavalry during the war and made sure everyone knew he had been in it. "Could at that, ma'am. You wanting me to charge him with anything?"

"Not unless you want to." Bearcat Annie was looking at Dusty with even more interest now. "The Town Council were a mite over-eager to take you on. I didn't get time to say if I approved."

"Your man came in and got out-voted, ma'am."

"So I heard. I sent another man down to the jail to ask you to come along and see me. He isn't back yet."

"Nor won't be, ma'am," Dusty replied. "He's in jail."

Bearcat Annie frowned again. Her eyes were not friendly as she looked Dusty over. "What charge?"

"I'm calling it disturbing the peace."

"He's lucky to be alive now," Mark went on. "Any man who tries to run a blazer on a lawman asks for all he gets."

The crowd stood watching everything. Bearcat Annie's place was not only the biggest and most garish in Quiet Town, it also was known as the toughest. Bearcat Annie herself was said to be the power behind the town and to have the ability to remove anyone who crossed her. They all waited to see how she handled those young looking Texans who now wore the badges of Quiet Town's police force.

"You like to take a drink?" she asked.

"Not while we're working, ma'am," Dusty replied.

"All right. The pickings are good for a lawman in Quiet Town. If he knows how to act. How much pay are you taking in?"

"Enough, ma'am. One rule I always learned. Take pay from only one boss at a time. That way a man lives to draw it longer."

"Dusty being brought up polite doesn't say it, ma'am," Mark went on, "but we don't take bribes."

Bearcat Annie scowled. There was real anger in her eyes although she held her temper in control. "You don't. That is a change among lawmen. I'll pay the fine for my boy. From now on don't put any man who works for me in jail. I don't like it."

"Ma'am, I'll jail any man I want," Dusty replied.

"If any more of your men try to run a blazer on me they're going to wish they hadn't."

The saloon owner watched the three young Texans walk from the room. She glanced at the groaning man Dusty had knocked over the table, then at the unconscious bouncer. With a contemptuous jerk of her head she ordered them taken out back then went up the stairs again.

On the street Doc looked at Dusty. "A man'd say you knew that big gent in the saloon."

"Was my farrier in the Texas Light," Dusty answered. "Say one thing, that blonde gal's real fast thinking."

"Meaning?" Doc asked looking at Dusty again, seeing far more than he had first realised. Dusty was more than just good with a gun.

"Like this. A lawman in any town stands or falls on the way the folks back him. That play there was rigged to try me out. Dammed near everybody who knows Cy Bollinger for over a week knows how mean he gets when he's riled. She figured that I'd either kill Cy, who never goes armed, or back down. Either way I lose respect of some of the town."

"Man'd say you gave her a surprise," Doc chuckled. "I know one thing. You sure handed one to me."

They arrived at the jail and heard a woman's voice raised in anger inside. "I'm warning you, Cy Bollinger. I've just about took all I aim to. Going in that fat hussy's place and getting arrested for brawling!"

Dusty, Mark and Doc entered to hear Bollinger spluttering feeble attempts at apologising while the big, buxom, good looking woman told him what she thought of him. She was a black haired woman wearing a cheap gingham dress which emphasised a figure as rich and full as Bearcat Annie's. Turning she stopped, then smiled a greeting at Dusty.

"Why howdy Cap'n Fog, sir." Her voice dropped to

a polite note which contrasted with the strident tones she had used to her husband. "I'm sure Cy didn't mean any disrespect down there. He was led astray by them evil bunch."

"That's all right, Mrs. Bollinger, ma'am," Dusty removed his hat and held out his hand towards her.

Maggie Bollinger rubbed her palms against her frock then took Dusty's hands, blushing in a manner which would have amazed her friends. She was never able to get used to a famous man like Captain Fog treating her with respect and politeness.

"How about Cy, Cap'n?"

"There's no charge against him. But Cy—."

"Yes sir, Cap'n," Bollinger answered, stiffening up again.

"You cause trouble again and I'll bounce you the length of Lee Street by the ears. Understand?"

"Yes sir, Cap'n." Bollinger had never really understood the strange fighting techniques of *karate* and *jujitsu* Ole Devil Hardin's Nipponese servant, Tommy Okasi, taught Dusty. What Bollinger did know was they rendered Dusty well capable of doing just what he said. "I'll behave."

"And I'll see that he does," Maggie Bollinger warned grimly. "Come on home, you."

Cy Bollinger followed his wife from the room still trying to explain how he came to be in Bearcat Annie's place. The door shut and Dusty looked at the others. "See what it's like to be married."

"Sure, that's why I'm staying single," Rusty agreed.

Dusty chuckled. He knew the Bollingers were a happily married couple and devoted to each other. It was only when something like this came up that their happiness was marred.

"How's the prisoner?" Mark asked.

"Bedded down real comfortable. The Judge came by. Says he'll be back to tell you how much the fine is, Dusty," the Kid replied. "That gambling man sure handles a real mean broom."

The jail was cleaner, the weapons in the racks looking more serviceable than before. Outside word was going the rounds of the town as men told of what happened in Bearcat Annie's Saloon. The general feeling was that at last Quiet Town was going to have some law.

CHAPTER FOUR

Roxie Delue

"I'll raise!" Mark Counter said the words of wisdom as he studied his cards. "And if you've got those three kings again I'm going to look on you with dire suspicion."

Doc Leroy, the dealer, shrugged his shoulders. "T'ain't worth me trying to put them back. I'd only have to get them out again next deal."

It was the morning of their second day in office as the law of Quiet Town. The town remained quiet for the night, people not wanting to be the first to try out those soft talking but fast moving young men any further. Word of who the town marshal was went out. The gun-handy men of the town knew Dusty Fog's reputation and were willing to wait for someone to go against him first. The miners, for the most part not gunfighters, were content to wait and see how he treated them. The rest of the town heard of how Bearcat Annie failed and stayed their hands, withholding any judgment until they knew what changes their new Marshal meant to bring.

Dusty leaned by the wall watching the poker game between his four deputies. Doc Leroy's slim, boneless looking hands were fast, he knew how to manipulate a deck of cards. By dint of fetching cards from the bottom, middle or just under the top card, Doc was winning. The jail was empty now, the gambler's fine having been paid he was set free.

The door of the office opened and a tall, slim young woman entered. Her hat was pushed back from her short cropped brown hair. Her face was tanned, pretty and without any beauty aids to try and make it look better. The buckskin coat could not hide the rich curves of her body. Her tartan shirt was loose fitting but the swell of her breasts forced against it. She wore a pair of tight fitting blue jeans, tucked into fancy decorated high heeled boots. Around her slim waist was a gunbelt with an ivory handled Navy Colt in the holster. The men looked at her, coming to their feet. Dusty was watching her face, reading something in it, a grief which lined her eyes and made her lips tight.

"Is this how the law earns its pay?" Her voice was a gentle southern drawl made hard as she looked them over.

"No, ma'am," the Kid replied. "We only plays poker when we're not sleeping. Which same's near on all the time."

"And while you're sleeping or playing poker folks are getting backshot in the hills."

The lounging manner left Dusty, and he came away from the wall. "Where, when, who and how?" he snapped, then before she could answer turned to his deputies. "Mark, Lon and Doc'll go with me. Go snake my paint out and saddle him for me. We'll pull out in five minutes. Now, ma'am, tell it, please."

The girl's face showed held down grief and her voice

fought to stay hard. "My pappy, over to Dutchy Schulze's place. I'll take you. Where's Webber at?"

"Who ma'am?" Dusty and the girl were alone now, Mark and the others having left to get the horses ready.

"The old marshal?"

"He retired. I'm the new marshal. You'd best tell me all you can as we ride out of town."

The girl looked Dusty over, comparing him with Webber. She looked around the clean office and knew that here was a man she could rely on.

"I'm Roxie Delue," she said and turned. "My hoss's out front, I'll get him and meet you on the street."

Dusty went out back to find his big paint stallion saddled ready and his short Winchester carbine in the saddleboot. The Kid was already afork his huge white stallion and Doc was swinging into the kak of his black. Dusty mounted his paint and grinned at Mark. "Don't let that big blonde gal scare you off, *amigo*."

The girl was afork a spirited looking bay gelding and rode astride with easy grace. She did not offer to speak as they rode from town, holding the horses at an easy trot. People watched them go by and there was some speculation about where the new Marshal and his two deputies were riding.

"Didn't tell me your name," Roxie Delue remarked.

"Dusty Fog," Dusty replied. "This's the Ysabel Kid and Doc Leroy."

The girl looked at him for a moment. She was a girl born and raised in the West and knew some of the top-guns. She knew that this small man was just who he claimed to be. Roxie felt relieved; her ride to town had been made with little or no hope of getting help from the local law. Now she knew that everything possible would be done to get the man or men who killed her father.

"Like I said, I'm Roxie Delue. My pappy ran a freight haulage company. We're only small, four wagons. We were up to Dutchy Schulze's place, just pappy and me this morning. We went to the cabin to call Dutchy and there was a shot. Pappy dropped. I didn't see who fired the shot."

"Your pappy have any enemies?" Dusty asked.

"A few. Some of the old timers. But they wouldn't go up against him from behind. They'd stack against pappy from the front. Besides, we've not been here long and none of pappy's old enemies are up this ways.

They were riding through the hill country now, the girl leading them along a winding wagon trail. Here and there could be seen the raw gashes and the tunnels of mines in the sides of the hills. Some of the mines were being worked, others stood empty and deserted. Faintly came the sound of an explosion as some miner blasted his way deeper into the earth.

"How about the gang that's been hitting at the other freighting companies?" the Kid inquired.

"For new boys you surely got to know things," Roxie remarked admiringly. "It might have been them but I don't see why. They tried to hit at us once. We've got a hard bunch working for us and we never run our wagons singly. Why'd that bunch want to kill pappy?"

"Be real stupid," Doc agreed. "Just to drop a man when there was nothing to steal from him."

"Maybe," Dusty said looking at the girl, seeing how she was fighting down her grief. "Figger it this way. This is the last freight outfit. With the boss gone it might fold up. Then the miners can't move their ore, can't ship in fresh mining equipment or supplies. Suppose there was another freight outfit waiting to come in here and take over. The hold-ups and the killing would make sense then."

"You could be right at that," Roxie agreed. "Without our wagons the miners would have been in tight by now. But I'm going to keep them rolling. Say! We had a dude come to see us just after we moved up here. Wanted to buy us out. Pappy told him where to go and he got uppy. Pappy showed him the business end of a Dragoon Colt. That ole dude took off fast, went faster'n I've seen anybody go since the day I dropped a live rattler on the floor of the school in Lil Rock."

"You know," the Kid remarked, guessing that the girl was holding her emotions in check and wanting to help take her mind off her troubles. "I figgered you were from Arkansas."

"And what's wrong with that?" Roxie bristled back.

"Waal, it warn't your fault you weren't born in Texas."

"It sure was," she replied heatedly. "I was three months late being born. All 'cause we were in Texas at the time. I just wouldn't get borned until we crossed the Arkansas line. I'd as soon been born a Yankee."

Dusty grinned at the girl. "Wall, I can't say Texas lost on the deal. See now why the Yankees never bothered to reconstruct Arkansas."

The talk died off for a time as they rode along. Dusty and the Kid were both noting where the various mines lay. They were town law and strictly speaking this was out of their jurisdiction. However they were taking a hand because there was no other law willing to do it. They might never need to know how the land lay around the town but if they did this would be a good chance to see some of it.

Roxie watched the men, knowing they were trying to help her forget for a time the deep and gnawing agony of grief which filled her. More to stop herself from breaking down than for other reason she started to talk. "We

were running our outfit from the Kansas railheads down
into Arkansas. Then some Pawnee renegades jumped us
and killed maw. Pappy was never the same after it. He
couldn't stand working in Arkansas any more and when
we heard about this strike we came up here. Was making
things pay us and now this."

Dusty reached over and gently squeezed the girl's
shoulder. He felt hard firm muscle in the arm and then
said softly, "We'll do all we can to get the man who did
it."

"I know that without being told," she answered.
"Don't worry. I'm not the crying sort."

They topped a ridge and she stopped the horse, her
breath drawing in sharply. In the valley below was a
mine tunnel and a small log cabin. By the cabin stood
a Conestoga wagon and in the small corral a team of
mules and a couple of horses. The girl was looking at
none of these, her eyes were on a blanket covered shape
on the ground by the wagon. She started her horse forward and the others followed her. The Ysabel Kid
scanned the rock strewn slope which rose sheer at the
other side of the valley. It would be a good place for a
man to lay up in ambush but he could see no one although
every instinct warned him all was not well.

Men came from the cabin, three of them, one behind
the other. The first was a tall, wide shouldered miner.
His hair was blond and cropped short, his face handsome.
He was a fine physical specimen; dusty guessed him to
be almost as tall as Mark and nearly as well built. The
man's cheeks bore small scars and Dusty guessed at their
cause.

Behind him came a short, scar faced Mexican wearing
the dress of the Texas border country and looking alien
in this northern range. He wore a gunbelt but the holster
and knife sheath was empty. Blood trickled from the

corner of his mouth and his face was bruised.

Pushing the Mexican forward urgently was a tall, dark haired young man. He was handsome, his face tanned by the elements and although it was a cheerful face there were hard, bitter lines to be seen by a man as knowledgeable as Dusty Fog. The young man wore a dark blue cavalry campaign hat, fringed buckskin shirt and trousers. Around his waist was a gunbelt, a knife sheathed at the left and an Army Colt butt forward at the right. He halted and looked at the newcomers with some interest, his hat coming off.

"Who is this, Miss Delue?" the big blond man asked, his voice having just a trace of an accent.

"The new town marshal, Dutchy." Roxie tore her eyes away from the still, blanket-covered shape.

"New marshal?" Dutchy Schulze turned and looked at the unarmed Mexican. "Then you want this man."

"Caught this rattler on the rim back there." The other man apparently decided he owed Dusty an explanation for his presence. "Was lining up on Dutchy here when I happened along. I brought him down here."

"Looks like he fell down the rim," Dusty remarked drily, looking at the bruised face. "Doc, you know what I want?"

Doc nodded. From his saddlepouch he took an oilskin roll which contained a small set of surgical instruments. A few years before he had been a medical student and now was frequently putting his learning to good use. He went to the blanket-covered form and lifted the covering up. With a bullet probe in his hands he set to work to remove the bullet, trying to prevent the girl seeing.

The Mexican stood silent and sullen. His eyes went to the Ysabel Kid with something like fascination in them. Then he lowered his gaze to the ground once more. Dusty glanced at the Mexican then to the buckskin-clad young man, taking in the Sioux moccasins on his feet. "Tell it, friend."

"The name's Day, call me Happy Day. I was riding scout for the Army until I came down here. Came up on the Mexican lining a Sharps on Dutchy here. Threw down on the Mex and brought him here. Me 'n' Dutchy talked to him but he's some quiet."

"Sharps, huh?" Dusty glanced at the saddle, laying on its side by the cabin door. It was a Cheyenne roll and a Henry rifle showed from the boot. "That your saddle?"

The Texans dismounted and left their horses standing free. Roxie swung down out of her saddle and faced the Mexican, her eyes hard. She did not speak but waited to see how Dusty handled the situation.

"Check the rifle there, Lon," Dusty ordered when Happy Day nodded.

The Kid went to the saddle and looked down. The saddleboot was made for a Henry rifle and would have been too short for a Sharps. Straightening up the young Texan returned to Dusty's side just as Doc joined them. Holding out a bullet Doc said, "Looks about right for either a Sharps or a Spencer rifle."

Roxie moved forward, her hand dropping to lift clear the Navy Colt. "You killed my pappy!" she hissed. "Who sent you to do it?"

The Mexican did not move or reply. With a gasp of anger Roxie lined the gun, her thumb easing back the hammer. Dusty reached forward and gently pushed her arm down again. "That's not going to get your question answered, ma'am."

The breath came from Roxie's lungs in a gasp. She still held the gun and her lips quivered as she fought down her desire to kill this man. The Ysabel Kid jerked his head towards the wagon. "Lash him to the wheel, then we'll make us some talk."

Dutchy Schulze reached out, gripping the Mexican and half carrying him to the wagon, slamming him against one wheel. Happy Day moved in, taking a rope from the back of the wagon and lashing the Mexican into place.

"Get that bullwhip, ma'am," Happy said, his voice gentle.

Roxie picked the long whip up, curling the lash in her hands. She knew how to handle a whip well enough. Looking at the blanket which covered her father's body she snapped. "I'll do it."

"It's no chore for a lady, ma'am," Happy answered.

Clenching her fists Roxie glared at the young man. She was close to tears and fought to stop them coming. "Don't you call me no lady. I ain't a lady and I'll fight the lot of you all at once or one at a time to prove it."

"Sure, ma'am," Happy Day agreed, taking the whip from her, his voice calm and gentle. "Maybe it'd be better if you went in the cabin for a piece, ma'am."

To the surprise of the other men, Roxie allowed Happy Day to take her to the cabin. Inside she threw herself on to Dutchy's bed and sobs wracked her slim frame as the reaction set in. Happy Day watched for a moment, then returned to the other men. He lifted the whip and brought the lash snaking out in front of him.

The Mexican still did not show a sign of fear. He knew these gringos would not kill him and the people he worked for would pay him well for his silence. He met Happy Day's eyes with a mocking sneer on his face.

"Blacksnaking won't make him talk," the Ysabel Kid remarked gently, coming to stand by the Mexican.

"Then turn him loose and I will break him with my bare hands," Dutchy Schulze suggested.

"Nope, that won't do any good, either," the Kid answered. "This here's a real tough *hombre*. He's from Sonora, ain't you?"

"Si, señor." The Mexican looked at this Indian dark boy, remembering something which made him more scared than fear of a whipping could.

"Them Sonora boys are all real tough, friend," the Kid's voice was mild. In his faultless Spanish he went on, "How do they call you?"

"Juan Sebastion."

"I am *el Cabrito!*" The Kid's voice was still mild. "Why did you kill the man?"

The change in the Mexican was immediate and a touching tribute to the reputation of the Ysabel Kid. There was real fear in the man's eyes and showing on his face. *El Cabrito* was a name to be feared in Mexico. It was not a name to give a prisoner joy or peace of mind.

"I don't know what you—."

The Ysabel Kid's right hand moved and the Bowie knife came out. "You boys just take a walk round the cabin there."

Dusty watched all this. He had seen the awe the Mexican border peons held his friend in. This one here certainly was in keeping with that awe. "No *señor*. No!" Frenzied eyes turned to Dusty. "You are lawman. You can't let them do it to me."

"Tell us what we want to know!" The Kid's voice was hard now.

"It was Bronco Calhoun—."

Happy Days moved forward, the hard, bitter lines more in evidence. "Bronco Calhoun?" his voice grated with hate. "You're lying."

"I'm not lying, *señor*!" the Mexican screamed. "Bronco Calhoun told me to kill the old man with the wagon. Then I moved around to try and get the miner."

"Where's Bronco Calhoun now?" Happy Day's voice still throbbed with hate.

"Up—."

A hole appeared in the centre of the Mexican's chest and the men heard the "whap" of a bullet passing. The group by the wagon hurled in different directions and a bullet ripped the heel from Doc's boot as he went under the wagon. The Ysabel Kid landed alongside Doc and cursed as he scanned the slope. High up, well out of pistol range he could see smoke rising and the shape of the rifleman. The butt of his Winchester in the saddleboot of his white stallion mocked the Kid. With that weapon in his hands he would either dislodge or kill the man on the slope. The other men were under the wagon with him and Dusty glanced as the Kid gave a low whistle. The white snorted and started to move towards the wagon. Then from the house came the crash of a shot and dust erupted just above the shooter. The man on the rim backed out and even as the Ysabel Kid dived forward to grab his own rifle the man passed over the rim out of sight.

"Want me to take after him, Dusty?" the Kid asked.

"Nope, he'll be long gone before you can make the top of the slope. You couldn't follow his sign over that rocky ground. Who was shooting?"

Roxie came from the cabin rubbing her shoulder. She'd heard the shots and used Dutchy's rifle, a long barrelled, bolt action weapon which she brought out with her. The rifle kicked harder than the Winchester carbine she had grown used to and the pain shook her out of her grief filled tears.

The men came from under the wagon and Dusty looked at the Mexican who now hung sagging in the ropes. "That's real good shooting," he said, bending forward.

A faint, elusive smell came to Dusty's nostrils and he leaned forward. The Mexican's clothes appeared to give off that smell but he could not place it. He looked at the Kid, before he could speak Happy Day asked, "Was he lying?"

"What about?" Dusty turned his attention to Happy.

"It being Bronco Calhoun he ran with."

Dusty shook his head. Although he came from the South he had heard some about the vicious old outlaw, Bronco Calhoun. The old killer was wolf smart and mostly ran with his six sons for a gang. If he took on extra help he used Northern men and yet the Mexican had claimed to be working with him.

"I don't know. What do you reckon, Lon?"

"I wouldn't believe one of his kind happen they told me Monday was a day afore Tuesday most times. But he was scared for some reason. He told the truth."

Roxie came closer, the rifle under her arm. She looked up at the rim and shook her head. "I allow to be better than that."

Dutchy looked at the girl, then at the rifle. "You used my Mauser?"

"Sure, sorry I did but my carbine's in the wagon. This damned fool rifle shoots high. I'd got the sights set for five hundred yards and it shot high."

"That was where you went wrong," Dutchy explained. "The sights are set in metres. On close range it makes little difference but it would at five hundred."

The girl handed the rifle to Dutchy and went towards the wagon. She glanced at Doc Leroy who was limping due to his high heel being shot off, then turned to Dusty. "Did he talk?"

"Some. Told us it was Bronco Calhoun who gave him his orders."

Roxie's hands clenched, quivering by her sides. Her voice was low and filled with concentrated, hate-filled venom. "The Calhouns did it. The greaser wasn't but a tool they used. I'm going to kill any and every Calhoun

I see. I don't care how I do it, but I will."

Dusty was watching the young Army scout. Happy Day's face clouded over with something Dusty could not tie down, some fleeting expression which Happy could not control. There was hurt in his eyes and he opened his mouth to say something. Then as if thinking better of it he closed his mouth again.

"Let us handle things here for you, Miss Delue," Dusty said. "Wait with the horses while we harness the wagon and load it for you."

The journey back to town was made in silence, the men all occupied with their thoughts and the girl not wanting to speak. Beside her, on the box and handling the ribbons like a master sat Happy Day, his face still showing the bitter lines.

Roxie watched Happy Day as he handled the team. For the first time she was realising the enormity of the task ahead of her. She was only nineteen and left alone in the world to try and keep the freight wagons running. It was the only business she knew. She also knew her father's men, reliable and old friends though they were, would never be happy without a man to lead them. Looking at Happy Day she wondered if he would stay on and help her. He was the sort of man she needed. He could handle a mule team and looked like a fighting man. He had been an Army scout which meant he knew Indians and other things a freighter needed to know.

Night was coming as they came into Quiet Town; the town was already loud and starting on the carouse which marked every night. No one took any notice as the wagon creaked along Grant Street and halted outside the jail. Rusty Willis came to the door, his face showing some slight trace of worry.

"Dusty," he said. "Mark just heard that Bert Calhoun's in Detard's place on Lee. Allows he wants to kill a Marshal and ole Mark's gone along. Left me here to watch the jail."

Dusty glanced at the girl, then snapped, "Doc, take Miss Delue to the undertaker's. Keep her out of it."

Roxie opened her mouth to say something, then closed it again. Much as she wanted her revenge on the hated men of the Calhoun clan she knew Dusty would brook no interference. She glanced at Happy Day, who was getting to his feet and swinging from the wagon box.

"You'd best go and help your pard, Cap'n Fog," he warned as he swung down and went to his horse.

The Ysabel Kid laughed. "I figgered old Mark's big enough to take care of his self and he's fair to middling with a gun."

"That don't come into it." Happy's voice sounded urgent. "Bert won't be in there alone. Your pard's going to be boxed in and cut down without a chance."

CHAPTER FIVE

Happy Day's Story

Mark Counter and Rusty Willis watched the others leave town then returned to the jailhouse. Mark picked up the scattered cards and returned them to their box and dropped it into the drawer.

"Ole Doc handles a mean deck of cards," Mark commented.

"A feller called Joe Brambile taught him," Rusty explained and darted a glance at the blond giant. "You've likely heard of him?"

"Some," Mark admitted briefly for the man in question did not have a good reputation.*

"Doc allows that all you hear about Brambile's not true," Rusty said coldly. "Anyways, ole Doc wouldn't use what he learned when he's playing for money—unless the other feller started it first."

*Doc's connection with Brambile is explained in: THE TOWN TAMERS.

54

"Talking of starting," Mark said. "Let's me and you give it a whirl now and start making the rounds."

The walk around town was uneventful until they reached the poorer class area. There they heard a disturbance in a house and went to investigate. A pimp was in the house, which was a small hotel in reality, and he was beating the girl who worked for him. Mark's handling of the situation was simple but very effective. Catching the man's arm Mark turned him, then hit him. The pimp went backwards, smashing into the window and going through, taking the sash and glass with him.

Mark dragged the unconscious pimp back to the jail by his feet. He was put in a cell and when, three hours later he recovered, was told he was being charged with disturbing the peace and damage to private property. He did not answer. His jaw was broken in two places.

The rest of the day was uneventful for a town like this. Mark and Rusty broke up a fight in a saloon, adding more prisoners to the unconscious man in the cells. There was a knife fight in a gambling house and Rusty showed that he too knew how to handle his fists, flattening one of the fighters while Mark dealt with the other.

So by the time evening came all was fairly peaceable in the town. A sense of trepidation came over the people, residents and visitors both. There were lawmen in town now, men who would back their play to the hilt. So, although the usual round of drinking, gambling and womanising started up at dark it was in a far quieter and less savage fashion than when Webber ran the law by sleeping in the jail.

Irish Pat came into the office, glancing at Mark and Rusty who sat playing cards before making a round of the town again.

"Where's Cap'n Fog?"

"Out of town on a chore," Mark replied. "What's wrong?"

"Bert Calhoun's down to Detard's place, at the far end of Lee Street. Bronco's oldest boy."

"So?" Mark was watching the saloon keeper's face.

"He says he wants to kill him a marshal."

Mark lifted the Colt from his right hand holster, checking the percussion caps were seated correctly. He holstered the gun again and checked his left. "I surely hate to see a man disappointed."

"What you going to do, Mark?" Rusty asked.

"Waal, killing a marshal's real hard. I'm going to let him get some practice on a deputy first."

"Want me along?"

"Not this time. He only wants to kill one of us. You stay here and watch the prisoners. If Dusty comes back tell him where I've gone. How'd you hear about it, Pat?"

"Word's gone round the town."

That did not surprise Mark who knew full well how news like that would get around. It would be passed from mouth to mouth, from bar to bar until everyone in Quiet Town knew a man was sending out a challenge. The town would be waiting to see if the gauntlet would be taken up and what would be the outcome.

There was nothing Mark could do but take up the challenge. Dusty was out of town and the sooner someone handled the challenger the sooner folks would know that law was here in Quiet Town. A lawman in a raw, wide open town could not let any challenge go unanswered. Not if he was to keep his self respect and the respect of the people in town.

Mark took up his hat and went to the door. "Stay on here, Rusty. Don't come after me. I'll handle this alone."

Rusty did not like the idea, he knew little of Mark's true capabilities with a gun. He had not seen Mark draw and wondered just how fast his tall friend was. However, Rusty knew the meaning of discipline and obedience to orders. He knew why Mark was going and why Mark needed to go alone.

Mark walked along Lee Street towards Detard's saloon. It lay on the edge of town, the last building on the street and was not one of the larger or better places. It was ideal for a man like Bert Calhoun, for after killing one of the town law a rapid departure was needed.

Mark walked through the streets at a leisurely pace. He was tense and alert for the possibility of a treacherous guntrap was not to be discounted. He could see people watching him from the saloons and other places he passed. Stepping up on to the sidewalk on the side opposite Detard's, Mark walked along until he faced the saloon. He did not waste time but went straight across the street and pushed open the batwing doors.

The counter was deserted except for a scared-looking bartender and a big unshaven man in dirty clothes. A man with a wolf-savage face and mean, hard eyes. His clothes were more of the northern ranges, and his gunbelt supported two Army Colts. It did not take a crystal ball to know this man was Bert Calhoun. Not when one could see the scared face of the bartender and the way the customers crowded into the far end of the room, well out of possible danger.

Mark was no fool, he'd learned the gunfighting trade well. He was not fool enough to walk into the lights of the saloon without taking some precaution. His deputy's badge was out of sight, hidden by the side of his calfskin vest. He saw Calhoun tense as the door opened, then the outlaw relaxed.

Bert Calhoun looked at the new arrival. He had heard how Dusty Fog was a short growed runt so this man could not be the marshal of Quiet Town. He also was not the sort to be recklessly challenged to provide proof of his identity. So Calhoun took up his glass of whisky and looked down moodily into it. Outside he heard the sound of hooves and wondered who was in such a hurry around town.

"Where the hell's that lawman?" he growled.

"Right here!"

Mark pushed his vest back, showing the badge pinned to his shirt and stepped from the bar. Calhoun looked at him, eyes wary, yet triumphant. The outlaw spoke, his voice harsh. "You ain't Dusty Fog."

"I'm not. Dusty's out of town. Being his first deputy I allowed to come here and save you from being disappointed."

"Did, huh?" Calhoun swung from the bar, hands lifting. "I wanted the marshal but I reckon you'll have to do instead."

Down lashed Calhoun's hands. At the same instant Mark saw a second big, unshaven man standing with hand on gun and knew he was in a trap. He saw it from the corner of his eye as his right hand dipped faster than Calhoun's grabbing fingers. The bar lights flickered on the eight inch barrel of Mark's Army Colt as it flowed from leather in that sight defying move of the true master. The web of his thumb was curled around and pulling back on the spur of the hammer even as the gun came up, his trigger finger pressing the trigger so that as soon as the gun was out and lining it was ready to fire.

The Colt, held waist high, lined with that unerring instinct of the true master, then roared. Calhoun spun around under the impact of the bullet and the other man lunged forward, gun coming up.

The batwing doors burst open, Happy Day came in fast, shouting, "Deke!"

Mark's second attacker hesitated, even as Bert Calhoun was dropping. He saw the buckskin-dressed young man and his face showed amazement. "Dayt—!" he began, trying to bring the gun round to line on this apparition.

Happy Day's draw was fast as he hurled himself to one side, the Army Colt roaring an answer to the bullet the man threw at him The man jerked back on his heels, then hunched over his gun falling.

Bert Calhoun was down but the wolf-savage breed like that died hard. His gun was still in his hand, and he fumbled to pull back the hammer. Mark acted as a trained lawman, his own gun roaring again. Calhoun jerked and the gun fell from his hand as the side of his head appeared to erupt.

Smoke rolled from two gun barrels. Two bodies lay on the floor, lifeblood pumping into the sawdust. Mark's gun was ready as he turned to face the room, he saw Dusty and the Kid coming through the doors and nodded to the young man whose timely arrival saved his life.

"Thanks, friend," he said, gratitude in his voice. "Sorry I couldn't wait to let you oblige him, Dusty."

Happy Day holstered the gun and went forward. There was something hard and savage about the casual way he rolled the body of the second man over with his toe. He bent down to make sure the man was dead, then holstered his gun.

Talk welled up around the saloon and the watchers crowded forward. Dusty looked down at the bodies, then his eyes went to Happy Day. "Like to see you down at the jail, Happy. You all right, Mark?"

"Why sure, don't know how I'd been if this gent didn't cut in."

"Dead, most likely," Dusty said. "Bartender, where's Detard?"

A slender, dark-looking gambler rose and came forward. "That's me."

Dusty's face was far from friendly as he looked the

man over. "Mark walked into a guntrap here. Did you know about it?"

"No!" Detard's reply was sure and his voice held a ring of truth. "Calhoun came in here alone. I couldn't let my bouncers stack against a man as good as him. I didn't know there was more than one of them."

The Ysabel Kid was looking the customers over, his eyes coming to rest on a familiar face. He crossed the room looking meaner than a *tizwin* drunk Apache, halting in front of Clint Fang, Bearcat Annie's topgun and boss dealer.

"You're feeding off your home range, gambling man," the Kid growled.

Fang looked up where he sat alone at a table. There was an uneasiness in his eyes. "Sure, came here to see how the law stacks up against a dangerous man."

"And you saw. He didn't do no better than you. At least he had the guts to push it through."

Fang pushed back his chair, coming to his feet in a lithe move. Then he stood very still. The Ysabel Kid's bowie knife was out, the point lined on his stomach and ready for a belly ripping slash.

The crowd drew back. They all knew Clint Fang was said to be very good with a gun. Fang himself thought so. Thought it very hard. Yet there was something in the red hazel eyes and the mocking Indian dark face that gave pause to him. Here was a killer, as near a Comanche Dog Soldier as a man needed to be to make him one. This was no fool kid dressed up and acting a part. He was the real thing and that bowie knife coppered the bet of any undrawn gun. Fang knew he was beaten from the start. Dusty Fog or Mark Counter would give him better than an even break but the Ysabel Kid did not have the same high-minded scruples.

It hurt to back down, for Fang was proud of his reputation. He knew he would be branded as a man who boasted and could not back his boast. That was very bad but it was not as bad as being ripped wide open by that eleven and a half inch of razor-sharp knife.

"Me, I didn't want to push nothing." The words were forced out, knowing every one would be repeated around the town. "I just happened to be in here."

"Well, just happen out again then." The Kid's knife went back as he spoke.

For an instant Fang thought of drawing, but those eyes never left his face. He knew the Kid wanted him to draw. He also knew that in his present state he could not face a fight. Keeping his hand clear of his gun he pushed by the Ysabel Kid and walked from the room.

Dusty watched all this without a word. It would do the law no harm for the town to know it was ready to back itself to the hilt against anyone. He gave his attention to Happy Day again as the buckskin-dressed young man spoke to Mark.

"You'd best watch your back now, Mark. Ole Bronco'll be looking for you and he won't care how he gets even. Bert and Deke were the only two of his boys who meant anything to him."

Once more Happy Day spoke with complete conviction about the habits of Bronco Calhoun. Dusty noted this but the questions which welled up in his head were not to be asked or answered here. "Let's go down to the jail, all of us."

Happy knew he was included and could guess what was going on in Dusty's mind. Walking to the door he wondered just how much trust he could expect from this soft talking, small man. He knew he was going to tell the truth and answer every question, after that it would be up to Dusty Fog to take whatever action he thought necessary.

The four young men walked from the saloon and as they started towards the jail they heard the sound of hooves as one of Buzzard Grimwood's hearses came from town towards them. They waited until it passed, then leading the horses walked back to the jail. The Ysabel Kid told Mark how they managed their timely arrival but Dusty did not speak. Nor did Happy Day.

The jail office was quiet when they returned and entered. Rusty and Doc were both there, the latter having taken Roxie Delue first to Grimwood's establishment, then to her home where her hired men took charge of the wagon and she went to get changed.

"Lon, take Doc and Rusty, make the rounds," Dusty ordered.

The Ysabel Kid nodded. "Sure. I'll put my hoss in the corral first."

Dusty and Mark remained in the office, they sat at the desk and Dusty waved Happy Day into a chair. "You'd better tell it, Happy. You sound like you know a tolerable amount about Bronco Calhoun."

"Yeah!" Happy's voice was harsh and bitter. "I know a tolerable amount about Bronco Calhoun. I should know. My name's not Day. I'm Dayton Calhoun. I was with ole Bronco for—!"

The door of the office was slightly open and a gasp sounded from it. The door was pushed open and Roxie Delue stood there. The Navy Colt was in her hand, lined on Happy Day, a look of hate on her face as she pulled back the hammer.

"Calhoun!" she gasped. "You're one of those Calhouns. Bronco's son."

The men sat without a move. The gun was lined rock steady on Happy's chest, the hammer drawn back and the girl's finger pressing the trigger. No matter how fast any of them moved they could not save Happy. The instant Roxie's thumb relaxed its hold of the hammer it would fall, strike and explode the percussion cap which would send its spark of flame into the powder in the chamber and hurl the .36 ball into Happy's body.

"Go ahead!" Happy's voice was barely more than a whisper. "That'll be three dead Calhouns for you."

"Three?" Roxie had heard the shooting and guessed some of what happened. "But Mark only went to find one."

"That's right," Happy's eyes were on the girl, pleading, not for his life but for her to believe and trust him. "Mark killed Bert. I killed Deke."

The gun wavered, the hammer lowering, although she did not holster the gun. "You killed your own brother?"

"Bronco wasn't my father, even though I lived with him for years. My mother and I were on a stage he robbed. He killed the rest and took us because our name was the same as his. I was eight and for seven years we lived with him. He tried to make me like the others but I wouldn't. Reckon I'm just stubborn. I was fifteen when Bronco's gang raided a bank and got drove off. Him and his boys got clear although they left five dead men behind. Bronco was mean drunk when he got back to the hideout. He blamed maw for the raid failing and shot her. Would have shot me too but his gun was empty. He pistol whipped me and left me there. Reckon he thought I was dead. I should have been. Two days later a couple of Sioux bucks found me. They were fixing to kill me but a man called Alvin Travis saved my life. He was a scout for the Army and couldn't have been kinder if he'd been my own father. He buried maw and took me with him. Told folks we were a nester family the Injuns got and that way they didn't get curious about me. I swore I'd get Bronco and every other member of that family. Alvin did all he could to help me. We rode together and he taught me how to drive a wagon team, and ride scout. He was killed a year back and I started out to look for Bronco. I know the way Bronco and his boys work so when I got word they were down here I came looking."

The room was silent when Happy Day finished his story, none of the others saying a word. Roxie's face was a flickering whirl of emotions as she looked at the young man she had meant to kill. The gun hung at her side unheeded until she remembered it and shoved it back into the holster. There was pity and shame at her own actions, on her face. She saw Happy looking at her and knew that bad as he wanted the Texans to believe him he wanted her trust far more. She felt something wet on her cheeks and reached up a hand angrily to brush the tears which welled in her eyes.

"Dang Texas tobacco!" she snapped angrily although neither Dusty nor Mark were smoking. "Those Tejanoes smoke the leavings of the trail herds."

"Sure," Happy answered with a grin at the girl, knowing he had gained her respect. "Those Johnny Rebs allus do some fool—ow!" The words were stopped by her stepping forward and kicking him hard across the leg. "What did you do that for, boss lady—ow!"

Roxie stepped back again from giving the second kick. "First time was for insulting us noble Confederates. The second was for calling me a lady."

"Sure Happy," Dusty agreed. "There ain't no ladies ever comes from Arkansas."

"How about Annie Breen?" she asked, mentioning the heroine of a folk ballad.

"Way the Kid sings it she came from ole Kentucky," Mark put in.

The tension was gone now, the men relaxed. Happy smiling as he watched the girl. Dusty and Mark rolled smokes and got them going although the smoke did not appear to hurt Roxie's eyes any more. Happy broke the silence. "Was I staying on here I'd need a riding chore."

"Could maybe take on another deputy," Dusty suggested, winking at Mark.

"And maybe you couldn't!" Roxie was bristling like an alley cat faced with a dog. "Happy don't want to associate too close with you Texas hellers. Besides," her face was flushed, "he don't want no deputy's chore when he can work for me."

"That's right," Happy agreed. "I'll take on with you, boss lady. If only to save you from these Texans."

"One thing, Happy," Dusty remarked, holding out his hand. "You're still Happy Day to us and the rest of the town. It might be better that way, folks wouldn't take kindly to having a Calhoun around."

"Yeah," Roxie gave her agreement. "What with one thing and another they'd be some riled I reckon. Specially with the way the gang's been hitting at the miners and the freight outfits. Come on down to the office, Happy. I can fix you up in with the other boys."

"Reckon we'd best start in to earning our pay, too," Dusty told Mark. "Let's go out."

They were making for the door when the Ysabel Kid, Doc and Rusty came in with a couple of prisoners. The men were pushed into the cells without ceremony and the Ysabel Kid told Dusty why they were being incarcerated. The men had been rolling a drunk and the Ysabel Kid left it to Rusty and Doc to take them. The Kid was quite satisfied with what he had seen and told Dusty about it.

"They're all right. Handled as neat as I've seen. Got their guns on those pair of rollers, leaned 'em against the wall and searched them. Give 'em a couple of days or so and they'll be set to work themselves."

Doc and Rusty returned from the cells after bedding down their prisoners and settling them in the cells. They looked at Dusty and he grinned as Rusty went to sit down at the desk.

"Mark, you and Rusty take a walk around the back, out towards Chinese Street. Lon, stay on as jailer and I'll take Doc."

The walk around the town was without event until they were walking back towards the town centre. Doc and Dusty came along the sidewalk, stopping to glance at the poster in front of the Beaumain Theatre. Then from across the square, at Bearcat Annie's they heard two shots, one light and the other heavy, the lighter coming first. A window broke on the first floor of the saloon as a bullet broke through it.

"Let's go!" Dusty snapped.

They crossed the street and pushed open the batwings, entering the saloon. All attention was shared between the two young Texans and Bearcat Annie who lounged by the bar. She came forward as Dusty and Doc crossed the room.

"Something for you?" she asked.

"Those shots up the stairs, ma'am. What happened?"

She smiled mockingly, jerking her hand towards the stairs leading to the first floor. A big, heavily built bouncer stood blocking the way up, another at the top, both looking down.

"Why don't you go and see?" Bearcat Annie asked.

CHAPTER SIX

Bringing In The Law

Dusty walked forward towards the stairs, conscious that every eye was on him. The customers at the bar and the tables, those standing on the verandah, looking down, all wondered how the small Texan would handle things. The bouncer at the foot of the stairs grinned as he measured the distance with his eye.

"Move!" Dusty snapped. "I'm going up there."

The bouncer moved aside with surprising mildness but as Dusty passed swung his fist. It was a good blow, struck with all his weight behind it, the fist ripping at Dusty's temple with enough force to fell an ox. It would have knocked Dusty unconscious, if it landed. Dusty's head went down, under the blow and the bouncer was thrown off balance. Coming up inside the man's reach Dusty brought up his hand, the heel smashing under the bouncer's top lip, crushing it. Never in a life full of being hit had the bouncer known such pain. His eyes were filled with tears of pure agony as he stumbled into a sitting position on the stairs. Dusty struck again, the fingers straight and tight together, the thumb across his palm to hold the hand rigid in the *tegatana,* the hand-sword of karate. Like a knife the edge of the hand slashed into the man's throat. The bouncer's head rocked back, and he was unable to breathe.

Without another look at the man Dusty went on up the stairs. The bouncer turned, his hand going towards his gun. Doc Leroy came gliding in, his boneless-looking right hand making a flicker of movement as his Colt cleared leather, rose then thudded down on to the bouncer's close cropped head. The man went down as if he was boned and in the same move Doc came round, his gun swinging in an arc which froze the hostile moves contemplated. Bearcat Annie's men halted their course of action. They had seen the speed and the way this pallid, studious-looking young man drew and handled his gun. He might not look much but he was the peer of any man in the room.

Dusty carried on up the stairs, ignoring what was happening behind him. He knew Doc Leroy was behind him and was confident in the slim cowhand. That left Dusty free to give his full attention to the man at the top of the stairs. The bouncer watched Dusty and, lifting his foot, tried to stamp at Dusty's head. Then he yelled, two hands caught his ankle, his leg jerked up, twisting it. He yelled again, lost his balance, hitting the banister and going over. Dusty gave no thought to the man, not even looking as the bouncer crashed to the floor below and lay writhing in agony, his leg broken. It was hard and savage but Dusty knew that in a town like this the law must be as tough if not tougher than the other side.

"Where was the shooting?" he asked, seeing the respect in the eyes of onlookers as they moved back to allow him passage.

Bearcat Annie stood watching Dusty go towards the room where the shooting happened. Then she looked at Doc Leroy who was standing with his gun back in leather again. "You boy badges are starting to rile me," she snapped. "You won't be so uppy if I have the boys throw you out."

"That's right, ma'am." Doc's voice was mild. "I wouldn't. But do you reckon your boys could do it— *before* I send a couple of forty-four balls through that fancy ole chandelier up there?"

The blonde woman's eyes left Doc Leroy and went to the magnificent crystal chandelier in the centre of the room. It was her pride and joy, the finest of its kind in Montana. She thought of what a couple of .44 would do to it and of how fast he could draw his gun. She *might* get her men to try to throw him out. However, she knew that not one of them could move fast enough to stop him sending lead into the chandelier and bring it down in a shattered mass.

Dusty opened the door of the room and entered. Some ten or so men were standing around one side of the long table in the centre of the room. On the other side facing them was a tall, lithe gambler with a keen, tanned face that was at odds with his profession. On the vingt-et-un layout, near his right hand, lay a Colt Army revolver. At the right of the table, face down and still, lay the body of a short, heavily-built man, a Smith and Wesson revolver clutched in his right hand, a pair of glasses by his side. There was not a mark on the man to show how he came to die.

"Tell it, one of you!" Dusty ordered, glancing at the window behind the gambler and the star-shaped hole where a bullet went through.

"He lost some," the gambler replied, indicating the body. "Was a poor loser. Started yelling that the deck was marked and went for his gun. Got off a shot and missed. I didn't."

"That's right, marshal," a storekeeper who Dusty knew slightly agreed. "This's Frank Derringer, he's a straight gambler."

"Call my deputy up here," Dusty ordered, looking at the small, light calibre Smith and Wesson then at the Army Colt. His eyes went to Derringer as a man left to carry out his orders. "Open your coat, Mr. Derringer."

The gambler opened his coat. He did not wear a gun-belt but under his arm was a device Dusty knew of although this was the first he had seen. The shoulder clip was made on a leather harness and with two U-shaped metal clips which would hold the chamber and the barrel of the gun. One glance told Dusty the clip was made for the Army Colt. Also that the harness would not fit the other man, so Derringer could not have changed weapons.

Doc Leroy came in, followed by Bearcat Annie. The woman looked around then snapped, "Keep your mouth shut, Frank. I'll get a lawyer here."

Dusty ignored her, pointing to the blue backed deck of cards on the table. "Check the cards, Doc."

"I run a straight game here, Marshal!" Bearcat Annie objected and there was no doubting her sincerity for once.

Ignoring her, Doc took up the cards, holding them to the light and looking at the backs. He tossed three cards on to the table by Dusty's hand. "They're marked. Look at the centre, the ink's darker there. It's real hard to see unless you look real careful."

Taking up the cards Dusty examined them. At first he could see nothing, then he made out the slight darkening in the centre. A man would have to be real keen eyed to see those marks unless he knew where to look.

"That's what they call daubing, isn't it?" Dusty inquired. "Hold out your hands, mister."

Obediently Derringer held out his hands, showing the fingers for, although he was honest, he knew how daubing was done. He also knew how easy a dauber could be identified. Dusty glanced at the thumbs, they were clean and unmarked so he went and rolled the body over, glancing at the bullet hole in the chest. Then he turned the left hand, on the thumb was a faint blue stain. Doc Leroy picked up the glasses, the lens were powerful, too powerful for any normal use. Handing the glasses to Dusty he pulled the man's waistbelt and exposed a thimble-sized metal pot filled with a thick blue paste.

"This's the dauber, Dusty," Doc said and went on to the gambler, "Reckon I was wrong about you, mister. I'd heard that Smith & Wesson go off first and when I saw the bullet hadn't gone through this *hombre* I figured you'd swapped guns with him afore we got here so it'd look like he started throwing the lead."

"So did I, at first," Dusty admitted. "Then I figured you'd not be using a full powder charge in your Colt, Mr. Derringer."

The gambler was at a loss to know what to make of Dusty. When he had seen the arrival of the marshal, Derringer expected either to be thrown in jail or run out of town. He knew his boss was not the best friend Dusty Fog possessed in town and would have expected the Texan to take advantage of this to get back at her. Instead Dusty seemed to have been working just as hard to find him innocent and justified in defending himself. He never loaded his Colt with the full, forty grain charge for use in the confines of the saloon. It would be dangerous to do so for the Colt would throw a bullet clear through a man and still retain enough power to go through the thin partition wall and damage anyone it hit on the other side.

Bearcat Annie was also surprised by Dusty's attitude.

He turned to her. "I'll send the undertaker along, ma'am, unless he's here already. How about your two men?"

"The doctor's tending to them. You play some rough, Marshal. We were only funning."

"Yes'm. I appreciate a sense of humour. Happen there's a next time I'll laugh good and loud. Then I'll close you up." Tipping his hat politely as he delivered the warning Dusty walked from the room, followed by Doc.

Dusty was puzzled by Bearcat Annie's attitude. The woman might just be trying to prove to him that she could run the town although a woman. There also might be some far more serious and sinister motive behind her <u>actions.</u>

At the jail Dusty found the cells were being filled up with sleeping drunks, crooked gamblers and various other miscreants. Mark turned as Dusty and Doc came in. "Got one I'd like you to look at, Doc," he greeted. "Put him in our quarters."

Doc and Dusty went into the room at the back and on the bunk lay the man who'd been in the poker game with them earlier. His face was pale and his breathing hardly noticeable; he was stripped of everything.

"Found him down in the Chinese section," Mark said as Doc bent to examine the man. "Couple of them were just taking his boots when we arrived. They took off and we lost 'em. You know what it's like down there."

"He's been drugged with butyl chloride," Doc remarked, straightening up. "Be out for some time yet. Keep him warm and he'll be all right, except for a bad head, come morning."

"Butyl chloride?" Dusty asked. "That's dangerous, isn't it?"

"Sure, unless the user knows how much to give and it varies with everyone."

"Then we've got to get whoever used it. Before they kill someone."

Mike, the miner, sat on the bed the following morning, holding his head. He glared at the door of the room wondering what all the noise was about in the passage. Outside, walking along the cell fronts, rattling a tin cup along the bars and giving wild yells, was the Ysabel Kid. Rusty Willis gave willing support and several of the prisoners joined in. It was Dusty Fog's special cure for drunks. At that hour, in the cold grey light of dawn, all someone who had drunk himself under a table the night before wanted was peace and quiet. The last thing he needed was for his aching head to be assailed by this noise.

The drunks were trooped out and sat on the bench in the passage, holding their heads. "Breakfast, gents," Mark Counter announced, entering the room followed by one of Irish Pat's men carrying a tray.

Each of the groaning men found a plate placed on their knees and eyes focused on their breakfast. There was a concerted rush for the door for a whisky-aching stomach could not face up even to the sight of cold, unsweetened oatmeal mush.

Mark watched the men staggering towards the water trough and grinned at his fellow deputies. "Here endeth the first lesson. Herd 'em back and get this place scrubbed out, then turn them loose."

Mike looked up as Dusty Fog came in. "What's happening, Cap'n?"

"Just seeing the drunks have some more fun. What happened to you?"

"That damned chippy!" the miner came to his feet, then realised how he was fixed. "Did they do—."

"Who?"

The miner told his story with many a lurid curse. He

had met a pretty young woman in a store and helped carry her parcels back to a small hotel where she was staying. There he had met her brother and been offered a drink. That was the last thing he could remember.

"We found you on Chinese Street," Dusty explained. "Reckon they left you up there knowing what'd happen. They figgered the Chinese would strip and rob you. That way you're not able to prove anything. They get much?"

"Couple of hundred dollars. I'll go down there—."

"You'll do nothing. I'll handle it." With that Dusty left the room, he sent Mark and Rusty to collect the woman and man from the hotel. They were told to search the room and see if they could find the bottle of butyl chloride. Then he called Doc and gave him orders.

Mark and Rusty returned with a voluble, protesting man and a soberly dressed, pretty woman. By the time they returned Dusty had arranged for clothes for the miner and brought him in.

"This them, Mike?"

"Sure!" The miner growled and lunged forward.

Mark Counter's arm shot out, thrusting the man back. Dusty snapped, "That's enough, Mike. Go get something to eat."

Slowly the anger left the miner's face, he knew that Dusty Fog was going to handle this matter. He also knew if he tried to object he was going to wish he never even thought of it. Without a word he left the room, shutting the door behind him.

"Found this roll of money, two hundred dollars," Mark said. "We near took the room apart but we didn't find the butyl."

"Then one of them's got it. Butyl's hard to come by so they wouldn't throw it away. We'll have to search them."

The man met Dusty's eyes, there was triumph in his

gaze. The girl, however, moved back, her eyes snapping fire. "You try and search me and I'll scream this place down."

"Reckoned you might at that, ma'am," Dusty agreed. He saw Doc returning and also saw he'd accomplished his mission. The office door opened and Maggie Bollinger entered, followed by Doc. "Howdy, Mrs. Bollinger. I need a special deputy. Pay's ten dollars a week. You take on?"

"Sure," Maggie looked at the girl and knew what her duties were going to be. "When do I start?"

"Right now. Take this lady in our room at the back and search her."

The young woman started to object but Maggie Bollinger gripped her arm and led her out of the rear door. Dusty took the man and pushed him into the cell lately occupied by the drunks. He searched the man although he knew there was nothing on him. Then from the other room he heard a slap followed by a harder blow and a thud. Leaving the man in the cell Dusty watched the drunks finishing scrubbing the passage floor. Maggie Bollinger came from the room holding a small green bottle, the girl was seated on a bed holding her jaw and crying.

Dusty went to the rear door and looked out at a small outhouse, a building meant as a grainstore. "Hold the gal here, Maggie. I'm going to get a jail rigged for her."

Dusty went back into the office and sent for a carpenter and Cy Bollinger to put bars at the window of the cabin. He then gave the now-sober drunks a warning which they took to heart. On returning to the living quarters, he found Maggie was thinking for herself. Her first prisoner was not in the room, she was scrubbing out her jail.

Doc Leroy and Rusty Willis managed to hide the

admiration they felt at the way Dusty Fog handled every problem which came his way. He appeared to have foreseen and have a solution to whatever came up. They had both expected trouble handling women and neither could have thought out a way to search the girl without laying themselves open to accusations by her. Dusty foresaw this same trouble and met it by bringing in a special deputy who could not only search another woman with impunity but could handle any violent objections to her searching.

In the days which followed they were to see and marvel still more at the way Dusty Fog handled the town. For a man who claimed that he knew little about being a lawman he made a fair hand at ad libbing his duties. Fights were broken up, the tough men handled by tougher methods. Doc himself inspected a gambling house and his findings closed the place permanently, sending its owner out of town fast. It also served as a warning to the other places, they never could be sure when that slim, pallid young man would make an appearance and uncover things which should have remained hidden from sight.

The drunks learned their lessons. It was far more pleasant to take less whisky and get aboard one of the wagons arranged by Dusty to tote them back to the mines than suffer the hospitality he offered at the jail.

In many things he stuck strictly to the letter of the law but one incident showed another facet of his character. It was on the early evening of their sixth day in town. Dusty was just about to send his first couple of deputies out when Maggie Bollinger arrived half carrying, half dragging a pair of dishevelled and dazed-looking young women of the class who could and did dare walk the streets after dark. She shook them into the chairs against the wall and stood between them as they sat crying and holding heads.

"They were fighting in the street outside the Beaumain Theatre," Maggie told Dusty. "It's not the first time that's happened. I banged their heads together to cool 'em down and brought 'em here."

"Put them in the women's cell," Dusty told her. He watched the girls led out and frowned. The girls worked for the two main brothels of the town, Jenny's and Big Liz's place. These two were the only establishments which sent girls on to the streets to raise customers. The Beaumain Theatre was a choice spot and although it had not happened while Dusty was in office, fights were common between the girls for possession of the highly-prized pitch. "Mark, go get Big Liz. Lon, bring Jenny in."

Big Liz and Jenny received the news that they were summoned to appear before the Marshal with some trepidation and the same thought in mind. They had heard of the fight and arrest of their girls and expected trouble. There was a group in town called the Civic Improvement Guild whose aim was to close every red-light house, and word had it they had seen the Marshal only that morning. With that thought in mind Big Liz pulled on her feather boa and told her bouncer to send her lawyer to the jail. Jenny thought things over for a time, then with a sigh stuffed a thick wad of notes into her reticule before going to join the dark, dangerous-looking young man who had come to fetch her.

Dusty sat at his desk and looked at the women as they stood before him. His grey eyes were far from friendly. Neither of the big, buxom women was easily disturbed yet there was something about this small man which made them uneasy. Big Liz looked out of the window in the hope of seeing her lawyer. Jenny opened the strings of her reticule and let the thick wad of money show while pretending to take out her handkerchief.

"Lon, keep everybody out of here," Dusty ordered

and the Ysabel Kid left the jail, shutting the door behind him. Maggie Bollinger went to stand with her back to the door, hands on hips.

"I want my lawyer before I say anything," Big Liz spoke first.

"You're not going to say anything, ma'am. I'm doing the talking, so lay back your ears and listen real good. You know why you're here. Two of your girls were fighting outside the theatre just now. It's not the first time that's happened. But it'll be the last. Seems like they can't decide who should be there. Nor can you. All right we'll let you decide. Maggie's going to take you out into the corral. The one who walks out gets to stay on and use the streets. The other gets out of town."

The two women stared at each other then at Dusty. Big Liz's voice was a worried croak as she said, "You mean fight each other?"

"Sure, just like your gals have been doing."

Once more the two madames looked at each other. The madame of a frontier brothel was of necessity tough, and both these were no exception. They were evenly matched in size and weight and both well versed in every dirty fighting trick. That was the trouble. They were too evenly matched. Neither one was sure of how she would come out of a fight with the other.

"You can't do it to us!" Jenny's voice was more of a whine now.

"Why not?" Dusty's voice was hard. "You send your gals out and let them fight."

Big Liz licked her lips nervously, Quiet Town was one of the best paying locations she had ever been in and she did not wish to leave. Neither did she wish to take her chance on a fight for she knew that whoever won would be in little better shape than the loser.

"Ain't there another way?" Big Liz asked.

"Why sure. Everybody knows where they can find your places. You don't need the girls on the streets. Keep them off. The next time I see one I'll close both your places and every other. If there's ever another fight between your gals you'll go into the corral." Dusty pushed his chair and stood up. "The next time I send for you, *if I have to*, don't bother bringing either your lawyer or bribe money. Neither will do you any good. Good evening, ladies."

Maggie opened the door and the Ysabel Kid lowered his foot to allow a thin, black dressed man to enter. "Captain Fog," the man gasped out as he came through the door. "I must raise a protest about the way your deputy—."

"Forget it, Louie," Big Liz cut in. "Let's get out of here."

Maggie Bollinger's face showed her admiration for Dusty as she prepared to go and check on her prisoners. "You done what you told them old biddies on the Civic Improvement Guild you would."

Dusty agreed with this. The virtuous ladies of the Guild had stormed in on him that morning with demands that the painted women were cleared out of town. They were routed and put into retreat by a young man who they had previously regarded as mild mannered and easy meat. They attempted to enlist the aid of Matt Gillem's wife but found her views on the subject matched Dusty's own. The girls of the streets supplied a vital need in this land of few women and many men. Neither the old woman or Dusty Fog approved of prostitution but they preferred it to the alternative. However Dusty was never happy about the girls being on the streets and pleased to have this opportunity to get them off without having to suppress them completely.

Walking to the backhouse now used as the women's

cell Maggie wondered on the complex nature of Dusty Fog and saw why her husband hero-worshipped him. He might not be tall, he might not talk loud but he was doing what three men died trying to do. He was taming Quiet Town.

CHAPTER SEVEN

Dutchy's Dilemma

Dutchy Schulze was a worried man as he rode into Quiet Town. He was so pre-occupied with his thoughts that he went by Dusty Fog and Mark Counter as they walked towards the Bonton Café for their breakfast.

"Hey, Dutchy!" Dusty called. "You getting so rich you don't talk to your old friends any more?"

Bringing his horse to a halt the German miner looked at the two young Texans. They had been in Quiet Town for three weeks now and although still no puritan Eastern city it was far tamer than when they arrived. They had seen something of Dutchy and Roxie Delue. The girl was still running her freight outfit with Happy's aid and making a go of it. There was no sign of Bronco Calhoun's gang and the miners were getting their gold out without loss.

"I'm sorry, Captain. I did not see you," Dutchy answered, holding out his hand. "I have worries."

"A man'd say you have," Mark agreed. "Man allus worries better on a full stomach and with a friend to help him. Come on in the Bonton and feed."

Dutchy was only too willing to go along with the two Texans. The problem facing him was enough to make him worry and he wanted to talk it over with someone. He fastened his horse to the hitching rail and the three men entered the café. They found an empty table clear of the others and sat down. After ordering a meal Dutchy looked at the other two.

"The gold vein the miners are working on is nearly played out."

"You sure of that?" Dusty asked.

"Sure enough. I am a trained geologist and know such things. Also at my mine the present vein is petering out even now."

"You say present vein. What's that mean?"

"It is hard to explain and I am not even sure that I am right. You see the earth formations are made like the layers of a cake. Between the hard layers we find gold. I believe that under the hard rock layer below this gold seam is an even richer vein."

They waited for the food to be brought and placed before them before going on with their conversation. Mark spoke first. "Why you so worried then?"

"It is very uncertain. There is only one way to find out and that is go under the bedrock and see. That takes special equipment and is not a job for one man. I can work my mine single-handed but could not with the new equipment."

"Hire more men," Dusty voiced the obvious solution.

"A simple answer to the problem. Unfortunately to hire men takes money. I have enough to make the deposit on the equipment and pay for Miss Delue to bring it here for me. I will have nothing left to hire men."

"Try talking to the mine owners, the big ones," Mark suggested.

Dutchy laughed. "I have tried but they say they cannot see an end to the vein. They have their shareholders to consider and don't want to waste money backing me on what might not even be needed. So I telegraphed to the mining supply company for the special equipment. The reply came yesterday. I am going to draw all my money from the bank and see Miss Delue."

Dusty looked thoughtfully at the big miner. Dutchy was sincere and appeared to know what he was talking about. However there was something troubling Dusty. "Have you told anyone about this idea of yours?"

"A few people. As I say, no one takes it seriously."

"Somebody might."

Ever since his arrival in town Dusty felt that behind every crooked enterprise, every try at keeping Quiet Town wild and woolly, every robbery or wrecking of a freight company, was one controlling influence. He could find no proof of it but on two occasions a lawyer was provided to try and help out some crooked operator taken to trial. Dusty also found out that several of the seamier and crooked places were not owned by the men who ran them. These men were mere employees for some person who even they did not know. The man behind the crookedness of the town would be interested in any news. If the original vein ran out the mines would go empty; then if Dutchy was correct there could be rich pickings for a smart man. If there was one man behind the lawlessness in town that man would have a very well organised spy system and probably knew of the message Dutchy sent and of the answer he received.

They finished their meal and Dutchy pushed back his chair. "Do you think I am doing the right thing?" he asked.

"I don't know the first thing about mining," Dusty replied. "One thing I do know is that if you know what you're doing you want to back it to the hilt. You get that special gear here and you'll likely find a man or two who'll help you and chance getting paid."

"Then I go to the bank and collect my money. After that I hope to get Miss Delue to leave today. The sooner I know for sure the sooner I can get the other miners to follow my advice."

Dutchy walked out of the room. Dusty watched him go then said, "Take after him, Mark. Follow him when he gets that money."

"Can't. I've got to take that pickpocket to court this morning."

Dusty came to his feet fast. "Pay the check," he said and left before Mark could either agree or object.

For once Dusty was in a hurry. He ignored the greetings of several friends as he made for the jail. He only just arrived in time. The Ysabel Kid was just leaving for a round of the town and the other two were already away. "Lon!" Dusty called and his friend halted. "Go to the bank. Dutchy's taking out his money, follow him and take care there isn't an attempt to snatch it."

The Ysabel Kid grinned. He had seen Dutchy in a fight and knew any man who tried to rob the miner was going to earn anything he got. However, one did not argue with, or question, Dusty's orders. It just was not healthy to do so. He turned and headed for the bank without a word. The Kid did not take kindly to walking which was one reason he was not fond of this chore they were doing. With typical cowhand thinking he hated any work that could not be carried out from the back of a horse. The duty of Town Marshal gave little chance to ride for most of the work was done on foot.

Reaching the street where the bank was situated the

Ysabel Kid saw Dutchy enter and followed. The bank
was a long, low stone building. Inside was the teller's
counter, a bench and a few seats for customers on this
side and Kennet with the two tellers behind the counter
and its protective grille. The bank vault and the office
where Gillem and Kennet conducted any private business
were beyond the stone wall behind the counter, both
strong enough to stand up to a charge of dynamite.
Around the wall of the bank was a verandah and on it
stood three shotgun-armed guards. They were on duty
all the time which explained why Matt Gillem's bank
never was held up. There was no way in except through
the front door and the room was covered by the well
armed men.

Leaning against the wall the Ysabel Kid removed his
badge and shoved it into his pocket. He watched Dutchy
talking with Kennet, then studied the other people in the
bank. There were not many at this early hour, a few
women, half-a-dozen men all strangers to the Kid. He
glanced from the window. Across the street a lean, cow-
hand-dressed man was leaning against the wall of a store,
smoking. He was paying just too much attention to the
front of the bank.

One of the men at the counter glanced at Dutchy who
was packing money into a note case, then strolled to the
door. He stepped out, removed his hat, mopped his face
then walked away. The cowhand tossed his smoke to
one side and stood erect, his full attention on the door
of the bank.

Dutchy walked from the bank, turning to head along
Bank Street towards the outskirts and the poorer section
of town. The cowhead followed on the other side of the
street and the Ysabel Kid drifted along in their wake like
a shadow. They left the prosperous business section behind and walked along through the poorer housing sec-

tion. Roxie Delue's freight company was based on the outskirts of town along this way.

The streets were deserted even at this hour, the women were doing their household chores and the children at school. The cowhand closed in, crossing the street to walk behind Dutchy. He looked back a couple of times but on neither occasion saw the Ysabel Kid who stepped into cover each time. The Kid was sure something was going to happen; it was a hunch and his hunches very rarely let him down.

Dutchy came towards a vacant lot, the cowhand moving in behind him, gun in his hand. "Hold it there!"

Stopping, Dutchy felt the muzzle of the gun touch his back. His hands lifted shoulder high for he was a prudent man and saw three more men coming towards him from the vacant lot, guns drawn. "You're wasting your time, boys. I haven't any money," he said.

"Yeah!" the cowhand replied as the other men, all dressed in range clothes moved in. "We'll see about it."

One of the men was about to step forward when he saw the lean, Indian dark boy across the street. "The law!" he yelled.

The Ysabel Kid never accounted himself fast with a gun. Not in a land where speeds of under half a second were regarded as fast. It took him almost twice that time to get his old four pound thumb-buster out and speaking. He flung himself forwards, hand twisting palm out to lift the old Dragoon gun clear. A bullet cut the air over his head as he landed and fired all in one move. The cowhand behind Dutchy reeled back, his gun falling. Dutchy was no coward; his bunched fist smashed into the side of one of the men's heads even as he was trying to cut down on the Ysabel Kid. The man, caught by the full force of the blow, was flung against the wall of the house at the edge of the vacant lot. His head smashed into the wall and he went down. The head hung over at an unnatural angle.

One of the other two men, a lean, unshaven north countryman threw a shot at Dutchy, catching him in the shoulder. Before he could fire again the man reeled under the impact of the bullet the Kid sent at him. He was still on his feet, even though hit by the soft lead round .44 ball. To the Ysabel Kid it meant the man was still dangerous so he lined and fired again, and the man went down as if he was boned.

The fourth man did not stay on to fight. He whirled on his heel and ran for it. The Ysabel Kid leapt after him, gun ready but the man went around a corner and by the time the Ysabel Kid reached it the street beyond was empty. The man was gone and there was little chance of finding him again.

Walking back the Kid found Dutchy bending over the man he had hit. The German's face was pale as he stood up. "He's dead."

"Good," said the Ysabel Kid, no moralist with a false impression of the sanctity of human life. "Let's have a look at your shoulder."

A small crowd was gathering, mostly women of the poorer kind, but Roxie and Happy came running from their office. "What happened?" the girl asked.

"Hold-up attempt," the Kid answered. "These three tried to relieve Dutchy of his wealth. Reckon you can fix his shoulder?"

"I was fixing bullet holes afore you was old enough to run contraband over the border," Roxie answered, recalling the days before the Kid met Dusty, when the Ysabel family were more than prominent in the smuggling between Texas and Mexico.*

*Told in THE BLOODY BORDER

Happy Day was looking at the Kid's second victim, his face hard. He went up and rolled the body over. Ignoring the crowd the Ysabel Kid joined the young man, leaving Roxie to take the wounded miner to her office. "You know him?"

"Yeah, it's Joe Calhoun."

"How about the other two?"

"Never saw them afore. But one of them looks like he came from your part of the range. Bronco never run with rebs, allus with Northerners."

The Ysabel Kid knew who Happy was, he also knew that these men were an unusual mixture. A Northern gang tended to keep to their own kind, so did the Southern men. Yet here were obviously a mixed gang, men from north and south working together.

The Kid waited until Dusty and the other deputies arrived. Doc and Rusty were left in charge while Dusty went along to interview Dutchy Schulze. "Pity you had to kill 'em, Lon," Dusty remarked as they walked to the freight wagon with Happy Day. "I'd like to know where they're hid out at."

"Out of town someplace?" the Kid suggested.

"Not likely, they'd have brought hosses with them so they could get away real fast. They're stashed away in town someplace."

At the office of the Delue Freight Company they found Roxie was making a fair attempt at handling the wound. The bullet went clean through without making any permanent damage and she was getting out bandages when the men came in.

"Happy, ain't it enough to make you want to spit. We've just yesterday took on to run them supplies out to Sand Creek and Dutchy wants us to go down to New-ton and bring some gear back from the railhead."

"We'll be back in four days or five at most," Happy replied. "Won't that do, Dutchy?"

"Of course," the German agreed. "I can wire off the confirmation to Newton."

"Dutchy." Dusty's voice was deadly serious. "From now on, until that money leaves, you'll have one of my boys with you all the time."

"That is not necessary, Captain," Dutchy objected. "There will not be another attempt to rob me."

Bearcat Annie moved among the early morning customers of her saloon. There were not as many in the saloon as before Dusty Fog took over as town marshal but she could not complain. She saw the door of her private office open and Clint Fang looked out, making a sign to her. She crossed the room and entered the office, shutting the door behind her. Fang jerked his head to a man who sat at the desk in the centre of the room. The man was breathing hard and looked worried. "How did it go?" the woman asked, glancing to make sure the big safe was locked up. There were things in that safe which not even Clint Fang knew about and which she did not want him to see.

"Bust!" the man who had escaped from the attempted hold-up answered.

"You mean you didn't get the money?"

"That's right."

There was worry in Bearcat Annie's eyes as she went to the desk and took the whisky bottle from the man. "All right. Tell me about it."

"Went the way you said it would. Dutchy collected his money from the bank, went towards the Delue place. We boxed him in and took him easy. Then that damned breed deputy jumped us. He dropped Tenspot and Joe. Dutchy got the other feller. I lit out, cut through an alley and come back here."

"Where's Dutchy now?" Fang asked, but the man ignored him.

"Were you followed here?" There was anger in Bearcat Annie's voice.

"Nope. I come real careful. Figgered I'd best tell you afore I went back to the hideout."

"You told me, now get back and keep out of sight. Tell Calhoun what happened to his boy but tell him to stay hidden."

After the man left by the rear door Bearcat Annie paced the room. The careful plan had come to nothing. The man who was the power behind her would not like it. She licked her lips and went to the desk, took a glass from the drawer, then poured out a drink. That mysterious man who ruled her and half of the town did not like failure. He would like even less seeing his careful scheme wrecked by those soft talking Texas boys who were becoming such a menace to him. Bearcat Annie was afraid her boss might demand Dusty Fog and his men were removed. She could not find the men in town who might be able to handle the task.

Slamming down the drink she cursed like a bull-whacker who had stubbed his corn-toe. Her boss, hearing of the message Dutchy sent and the answer guessed correctly how the German would react. His plans depended on Dutchy not being able to get the necessary equipment.

"Who're we working for, Annie?"

Bearcat Annie looked at Clint Fang as he spoke. "Meaning?"

"That fellow who comes to see you sometimes. The one we never get to see. I don't reckon he's just an admirer." Fang grinned at the woman. "I also guess you ain't the big augur of the outfit. Who is he?"

"Are you just asking, or do you really want to know?"

Fang closed his mouth hard at the concentrated venom of the words. He could read the signs and knew that here was something he had better stay clear of. He was on dangerous ground for since his failure to face either Dusty Fog or the Ysabel Kid he was no longer the most popular man in Bearcat Annie's crew.

There was a knock on the office door and Bearcat Annie called for whoever it was to come in. One of her barmen entered, followed by a thin, ratfaced dude in a loud check suit. He was holding a big, oily cigar in his left hand as he came towards the woman. His accents were New York, and East-side New York at that, as he greeted her. "Are you the boss here?"

"That's right. Who are you?"

"Joe Mundy, you sent for my troupe to come along."

Bearcat Annie managed a welcoming smile. Mundy ran a rugged kind of entertainment which she thought would go down well with the customers and she had sent for him to come. Her mind was not really on the man at all. "I want your best two gals tonight. You understand that?"

"Sure, I've got Olga Petrosky and Eeney Haufman for you. They're the best in the troupe."

Still Bearcat Annie was not fully listening but two words caught her attention. "You said Eeney Haufman. Is she German?"

"Sure. She's the top—."

"Those girls of your'n obey orders?" she cut in with more interest than she had previously shown.

"Sure they will. What do you want?"

Bearcat Annie looked relieved as she showed Mundy out of the room. There was a chance, only a small chance but one for all of that, if Dutchy accepted her invitation and was as proud of his country as she thought he might be. Fang watched her face for a time, he could see she was pleased with something but was not sure just what it was. Bearcat Annie went across the room to where Frank Derringer was playing solitaire. He looked up as she came towards him and nodded a greeting.

"Say, Frank. I've been thinking, Captain Fog isn't such a bad gent after all. How about going down to the jail and asking him if he'll come along to see the show tonight as my guest."

"Sure, Annie," Derringer was surprised at the woman's change of heart. "I'll go and ask them."

Derringer left the saloon and returned soon after with news which both pleased and amused her. She had guessed that Dusty would keep a close eye on Dutchy and this was confirmed when Derringer returned.

"I saw Dusty. He'll come and his boys. Dutchy Schulze was there and I asked him to come along. He's been shot in a hold-up attempt but he's all right and he'll be coming with them. Hope you don't mind."

Bearcat Annie most certainly did not mind. She knew Dusty would never allow the miner to go unguarded and this was the only way she knew to get Dutchy here so she could try and put her idea into operation. Bearcat Annie returned to her office and started to make her plans, showing a keen insight into the way men thought. She rose and went to the door to call one of her less scrupulous house gamblers in to give him his orders.

CHAPTER EIGHT

Bearcat Annie Entertains

The law of Quiet Town was preparing for its first night of relaxation since taking over. Of all the young Texans only Dusty was worried by the invitation extended to them. He was concerned about Bearcat Annie's change of heart for although there had been no further trouble with her he did not think she was the sort calmly to forgive and forget.

"You still worrying about her sending for you, *amigo*?" Mark Counter asked, for he knew Dusty very well.

"Just a mite. You know me, I'm naturally suspicious."

"Sure. It's a good way for a man to be at times. We haven't taken time off since we came here and I reckon the boys want a chance to relax."

Rusty Willis and Doc Leroy came from outside where they had been washing. They were getting worried about the non-arrival of the rest of the Wedge crew and deciding whether they should stay on for a spell or head down to Newton and find their boss. The decision was put off until after the evening out, and with Dutchy Schulze escorted by the five young men all headed for Bearcat Annie's.

The saloon was well crowded as they entered. Bearcat Annie herself came across the room, smiling a welcome and cutting through the crowd like a clipper ship going through Mississippi flatboats. Word that she was running some very special surprise entertainment was going the rounds of the town and the big bar room was crowded out. In the centre of the room was a raised square platform with a wooden post at each corner and three ropes running from post to post around the square. On the wooden boards which formed the base of this platform was a canvas tarp, in two of the corners formed by the posts were stools.

"What's that thing?" the Kid asked, noting how all the tables were arranged around the platform.

It was Mark who supplied the answer. "They call it a ring. I saw one in New Orleans while I was there one time. Use it for fist fights, looks like that's the surprise Bearcat Annie's got on."

"Howdy Captain Fog!" Bearcat Annie reached them, smiling in welcome, the flat meaningless smile of a professional entertainer. "I'm pleased to see you here. Make yourself at home. I've told the bartenders your money is no good tonight. You're my guests. Come on, I'll take you to your table."

"Was I a suspicious man I'd wonder about your change of heart, ma'am," Dusty remarked as they walked through the crowd side by side.

"Was I a more sensitive woman I'd be riled at your suspicions," she countered. "I'm not, so I'll explain. Sure, we've had our differences. I wasn't sure what sort of lawman you'd make, so I tried you out. I didn't want a fast gun, hired killer here running the law. Now I know I was wrong and when I make a mistake I'm the first to admit it."

The excuse was reasonable and yet Dusty was not fully convinced. It did not fall in with the idea he had formed of Bearcat Annie, that she would ever admit to making a mistake. However, there was nothing to be gained by antagonising the woman until she gave cause for it.

They were taken to a table next to the side of the ring, obviously a place of honour. Mark took a seat with his back to the ring and the others sat in a circle around the table. Dusty held out the chair for Bearcat Annie, then took a seat at her right. Dutchy Schulze pulled a bottle from his pocket, a square-faced bottle with a colourless liquid in it. "With no disrespect, Annie," he said. "I would like to let my friends try a drink of this."

Bearcat Annie laughed and waved off any idea that she might be offended. She beckoned and a waiter materialised by her side, carrying a tray with a bottle of her best bonded whisky and seven glasses. Dutchy poured three fingers of his liquid into each glass, then lifted his glass.

The others all drank; the drink might look like water but it packed quite a kick to it. Mark Counter coughed and rubbed his eyes then grinned admiringly at Dutchy. "Man, that's real likker. It'd curl the hairs on a mule-skinner's chest!"

Rusty Willis shook his head as the bottle was offered to him again. "Not for me thank you. What is it?"

"Schnapps," Dutchy replied.

"Kicks like that bottled bullwater Pasear Hennessey sells down at his place," the Kid remarked. "Knowed a man once drank three bottles of that and never staggered."

"Must have been some drinking man," Bearcat Annie

put in, determined to keep up the friendly atmosphere. "Three bottles, then never staggered."

"No, ma'am. He just couldn't move at all."

Dusty joined in the laughter and glanced around him. At the table behind them, almost in touching room of Dutchy and himself sat several loud-dressed gamblers who he knew worked for Bearcat Annie. The others around however were occupied by miners or the other customers. None of the nearby tables held anyone who might be a hired gun ready to take some treacherous action.

Kennet came by the table and stopped to greet the lawman. "Good work your men did in stopping that hold-up man, Captain."

"That's what they're paid for," Dusty replied, looking at the Kid and Rusty who were the men involved in stopping a man who held up a big stake private poker game.

"What amuses me is that at least three of the men were really good with their guns," Kennet went on.

"What's so funny about that?" Mark asked.

"But one man took their money. One lone man."

"With a gun." Dusty reminded the young banker. "Tell you something. If I was a hold-up man I'd sooner take Ben Thompson, King Fisher, Clay Allison or Wes Hardin than four ordinary men. Real good guns know what risks they can take, they've more sense than buck odds. Your real good man is safer to rob than a half-trained dude. *As long as you don't make a mistake."*

Kennet digested this piece of information. He could hardly believe that a man who was really good with a gun would sit mildly back and allow himself to be robbed. It was true, the good man with a gun would have more sense than buck the hold-up man. It was the dude who possessed that little knowledge who was dangerous, he might do something silly.

Passing on, Kennet went around the ring and out of sight. The talk at the table was general for a time then Bearcat Annie saw Mundy crossing the room and entering the ring. She pushed back her chair and stood up. "I've got an announcement to make, boys."

The men started to get up and she waved them down again, then walked around the ring to climb up and duck between the ropes. Talk welled up in the saloon and there was an air of expectancy through the room. Bearcat Annie waved for silence, then announced. "Boys! Tonight I've got you the greatest attraction you've ever seen. All the way from the East—." Six women walked through the crowd towards the ring, four in dresses, the other two draped around with long silk robes. They climbed the steps into the ring, the brunette in the robe and two of the women in the dresses going across to one corner. "For the first time in Montana Territory!" Bearcat Annie went on, ignoring the rumble of talk which was going up, "we have an all-woman bout of fisticuffs. Not only that, but this is for the Championship of the World. Over there we have the Woman Fist-Fighting Champion of the World, Russian Olga Petrosky." The blonde woman removed her robe and stepped forward to yells and whoops of delight. She was a woman of about five foot six, her face coarse and her figure heavily built. She wore a pair of black tights and a scarlet-spangled, sleeveless blouse, her fat figure straining at it as she acknowledged the yells of the crowd. "And the challenger!" Bearcat Annie went on, "Eeney Haufman of Germany."

Dutchy looked up with interest as the brunette woman tossed aside her robe and stepped forward. She was as tall as the blonde but not so heavily built. Her hair was cut fairly short and framed a face which, while not being out and out beautiful, was still pretty. She wore the same style of dress as Olga but her figure was far more suited to it. She also acknowledged the cheers of the crowd and went back to sit on the stool in the corner. She was in the corner nearest to Dusty's table and as men crowded forward to the ringside around Olga's corner, Dutchy rose and went to look at the other girl. In German he asked, "Where do you come from?"

Eeney looked down, seeing a handsome man with one arm in a sling. She was used to men speaking to her but this was the first of her own countrymen. She tried to read from his face whether he approved or disapproved of her way of making a living. "From Stuttgart," she replied, smiling down at him.

"Will you win?"

"Of course," Eeney answered, giving the usual answer although she knew Olga was to win.

"Then I will bet on you. Good luck."

Watching him walk away Eeney felt worried. She sat back with two of the other members of the troupe acting as her seconds. Bearcat Annie was telling the crowd the rules governing the fight and Eeney watched Dutchy return to his table.

"Tell you that German gal's got no chance."

Dutchy looked at the speaker, one of the gamblers seated on the next table. "Are you sure of that?" the miner asked.

"Sure enough, Dutchy. Give odds of two to one that she loses."

"I'll take the odds. A hundred dollars."

Eeney felt relieved at this; the words came to her and she doubted if a hundred dollars would break the miner. Then she heard the gambler laugh mockingly.

"That's a powerful lot of belief you've got there, Dutchy. All of a hundred dollars. Still, I reckon you know what the German gal's worth."

Dutchy was proud of his German nationality. Although he was not sure he approved of the girl being dressed in that manner and fighting, he did know she must have some sign of his support. Without thinking of the consequences he asked, "Will you take four thousand dollars?"

The gambler pretended to edge, following the instructions Bearcat Annie gave him. "That's a lot of money, Dutchy," he began. "I'd take you up but I work for the house and I don't know if—."

"Put up or shut up!" Dutchy barked.

Clint Fang arrived. "What's the trouble?" he asked.

"Dutchy wants to take four thousand on the German gal winning," the gambler explained. "I ain't sure if I should."

"I said put up, or shut up," Dutchy snapped, knowing that not only the five Texans were watching him but also that the girl's eyes were on him. He pulled out his wallet and tossed it on to the table in front of the other man. "Is it a bet?"

"It's a bet. You forced me into it."

"Can you pay off if you lose, friend?" Dusty asked; he was worried for he did not like to see Dutchy taking such a rash bet. It was, however, against his code to interfere with what another man did with his money.

"He works for the house," Fang put in. He should have kept out of it but his dislike for Dusty Fog made him speak.

That settled the matter for it was the custom of the saloon to employ professional gamblers to take bets from any client who wanted to get in on the action. The gambler was covered against his losses by the house and his take went to it. So there was no objection from Dusty as the gambler made out a receipt of the bet and gave it to Dutchy.

Bearcat Annie climbed from the ring and went to the bar, going around it to climb up and sit on a chair on the bartop. The two women in the ring advanced on each other, fists clenched and held up in the manner of professional pugilists.

Mark Counter turned with his back to the others and watched with critical eyes. He knew much about the fist fighting game, having learned it from his father's cook who had fought in the prize ring. The two women shaped up as if they knew what they were doing. He compared them with the view to betting although he doubted if this would be a serious fight. His suspicions were confirmed when the first blows were struck. They looked hard but he could see both women were pulling their punches. It was well done and he doubted if many people would spot it. Certainly the uncritical bloods in the crowd did not. Mark looked at the German girl, seeing the play of muscles as she moved. The blonde might have the advantage of weight but in a serious fight Mark would have bet on Eeney.

Eeney Haufman was worried as she toed the line. She had seen and heard how much the German miner bet on her and did not like the idea. For the most part the girls of the troupe followed a certain pattern in their fights, learning a routine which they could use without injury. The result of every fight like that was arranged and tonight Olga was to win. With the other girls it would have been easy, a word in the ear and the routine changed so Eeney won. Olga was the manager of the troupe's favourite, nasty tempered and a bully. She and Eeney were not friends and so Eency knew Olga would hardly be likely to agree to losing. She never did if she could help it, not unless they were laying a trap for a sucker bet.

Clinching Eeney tried to persuade Olga. "Look, Olga.

I want to win tonight. Can I?"

"No!" Olga hissed back, grinding her fists hard into Eeney's side. "Sorry, it was an accident."

Mundy pushed at them, trying to separate them and growling a warning. Eeney still hung on. "I'm going to win!" she hissed.

Hate glowed on Olga's eyes and she answered, "If you can!"

Mundy pushed the two women apart. Instantly Olga smashed her right into Eeney's body in a hard punch that brought a gasp of pain. Instantly Eeney hit back, feeling her knuckles grind into the blonde's coarse face. They circled, anger in their eyes and both knew it was to be the real thing this time, there would be no punch pulling or routine following.

Eeney bored in, her right stabbing into Olga's face, then her left driving into the fat throat. Olga stepped back, her own fists smashing into the German girl just below the breast and bringing a grunt of pain. Mundy circled them worriedly; he could see the blows were landing hard and did not like it. There were other times when two of the girls lost their tempers and really fought. They cost him money for the girls involved were usually in no shape to appear again the following day and Mundy was hired to provide a fight a night for a week. He tried to get between the two women without arousing the suspicions of the crowd and caught a punch from Eeney which knocked him out of the way.

The crowd were wild with delight; they had most of them seen hair-tearing fights between dancehall girls but this was a novelty. The two women were more scantily attired than was usual even in the wild, wide open towns and they were both an eye-catching sight for men who saw few women.

The first round was hard as the two women worked

their anger out on each other. Eeney ripped a punch up which caused a trickle of blood to run from Olga's mouth, then she gasped as the blonde's fists caught her in the stomach. She doubled over and saw Olga's knee smashing up at her face. Eeney jerked erect in her attempt to avoid the knee and tripped, falling backwards on to her rump. For a moment Olga stood looking down at her then turned and walked back to her corner. Eeney got up and returned to her own corner. She sat on the stool and the two girls started to work on her. "What's the game?" one asked. "You and Olga's hitting like you meant it."

"We do!" Eeney touched her lips which felt swollen. "I'm going to win tonight."

"Mundy said Olga was to win," the second reminded Eeney. "He isn't going to like it if she doesn't."

Eeney did not care what Mundy liked. She was not worried by the prospect of a serious fight with Olga and in fact rather welcomed it. The blonde was Mundy's favourite and no love was lost between her and the other girls. Eeney was not afraid of fighting seriously. There were other troupes of girl fist fighters going the rounds and Eeney in the two years she had been with Mundy had fought several real fights. She knew that Olga had also fought seriously and would take some beating. Glancing down she saw the German miner waving to her and smiled back at him, then time was called and she went forward.

Olga attacked immediately, lunging in with hard fists ripping at Eeney. The German girl rocked under the impact then her own fists started to score. Three times she felt her knuckles catch Olga's cheek, rocking her head, then the right came across. The punch was timed beautifully, Olga's head snapped to one side and she hit the ropes. Coming off the blonde threw her arms round

Eeney and started to hug her in a brutal crushing move. The rules of barefist boxing were far more lax and allowed things which were later barred from boxing. Olga was in her rights to use this crush and she put the pressure on, feeling Eeney's firm body fighting against her and the breath being forced from Eeney's lungs. Suddenly Olga let loose and Eeney staggered back. The blonde followed her and while she was still off balance brought round and down a smashing left which laid Eeney on the floor again.

"Your gal's not doing so good, Dutchy," the Kid remarked as he sat back and rolled a smoke.

"It's early yet," Dutchy answered. "You watch her."

Mark was watching, mildly surprised that the women were really fighting. He saw the way the referee was fussing around and guessed that this fight was not going to plan.

From her place on the bar Bearcat Annie was also watching everything and so far was not worried. She could not tell at this distance that the girls were not following the plan and thought their faking was well done. The first inkling she had of trouble was when the next round started and in a fast exchange of blows in the ring centre saw Olga rock back on her heels with blood running from her nose. Bearcat Annie slid down from the bar, showing a pair of shapely legs but no one was looking. She crossed the floor and from the tense, angry looks knew the two women were really fighting. There was no play acting in the way their fists landed on each other and the angry grunts and squeals were not faked.

"Great fight, Annie!" an excited miner said as she went by.

"Yeah, great!"

Bearcat Annie grunted the reply as she saw Eeney butt Olga in the stomach then rip up a punch that straightened the fat girl. Olga was wobbling on her feet, head spinning. She was wide open to the right Eeney smashed at the side of her jaw and went down hard.

At a table she was passing Bearcat Annie stopped by Soehnen and others of the big mine owners. They were valued customers and Annie knew she would arouse suspicions if she did not stay and talk with the men. They were all praising her for the inspiration which brought in the women fist fighters. The fourth round started with Olga getting the worst of a hard slugging attack and Bearcat Annie was forced to stand there, writhing in an agony of suspense while Eeney battered the blonde around the ring. Olga was tottering and looked about done as she sank to her knees.

"What's wrong?" Bearcat Annie growled, climbing on to the ring and holding a drink to Mundy. Miners were offering Olga drinks although Eeney was left free of their attentions.

"Eeney wants to win tonight for some reason," Mundy replied. He knew the saloon keeper wanted Olga to win but thought it merely so that she could tell her man to lay odds.

"Tell her she can't." Bearcat Annie could see her carefully arranged plan failing. "What started it?"

"Some miner bet a wad on her and she thinks he'll be bust if she loses." Mundy had taken the precaution of finding out.

"Go tell her he's the richest man in town. Could afford to lose it all and think nothing of it. Tell her we'll let her fight again before she goes and let him win his money back then."

"She wouldn't believe it."

"She'd better, or you bunch won't get paid."

Bearcat Annie turned and walked away, the man stared after her, then went to talk to Eeney. The brunette frowned; she did not like what she was told and did not believe that Dutchy would get a chance to win his money back. She glanced at him, he certainly looked wealthy and he was with the town lawman. She knew that many town marshals played attendant to rich miners and thought that Dutchy could afford to lose. Her job was at stake, Mundy made that clear. She knew that in the West there were few things a young woman with morals could do. Fist fighting in the saloons was not a ladylike thing, but it kept her and she was never troubled by unwelcome attentions.

"Tell Olga to go back to the routine," she said. "We'll carry on with it."

Mundy crossed the ring and looked at Olga. The blonde was gasping for breath and her face was marked. There was a nasty gleam in her eyes as she got up but she went into the routine once more. She was not so willing to make a serious fight of it since taking some of the punishment Eeney handed out.

Mark was watching every byplay and he saw the change in the way the two women went at it. Once more they were pulling their punches and although the fight looked just as rough he could tell there was little damage being done. Three rounds of this play acting followed and Eeney went into a routine long rehearsed. Olga sent a punch that looked as if it was meant, right into Eeney's stomach. The German girl gasped and doubled over in a realistic manner. Olga interlaced her fingers, got her cupped hands under Eeney's chin and heaved. Eeney went backwards as if out of control, hit the ropes and fell right over, out of the ring. She landed and by a chance was at Mark Counter's feet. He bent and lifted her up in his arms, putting her back on the apron of the ring.

"Ma'am, if you lose this fight ole Dutchy's going to lose everything he's got."

Eeney, eyes closed and face twisted as if in pain,

heard the soft spoken words and opened one eye. She looked at the handsome face and knew this Texas man knew what was happening. She also knew he was not lying to her. Anger flooded her as she realised that she was being made a fool of by Mundy.

According to the arrangement for that part of the fight she should stagger out and Olga would finish her off. Her seconds worked on her, they could feel her trembling and breathing hard. Time was called; Olga came out with confidence to get the shock of her life. Eeney came forward and smashed a punch at the side of her jaw which knocked her into the ropes in a heap. She hung there, half in and half out of the ring, tangled and helpless. Eeney came at her and Mundy yelled, catching the German girl's arm. Eeney turned and to the crowd's delight her fist smashed into the man's face and knocked him staggering. The other girls of the troupe ran forward catching Eeney and dragging her back to her corner. Then Olga's seconds helped her back and sat her down. A man from the crowd gave Olga a glass of whisky and she drank, or appeared to drink it just before she came out for the next round.

Eeney advanced with fists raised. She watched Olga staggering and made a bad mistake. Thinking Olga was hurt Eeney relaxed, then the blonde spat the whisky from her mouth into Eeney's face. The German girl was blinded for an instant and the whisky stung her eyes. Unable to see, Eeney was at Olga's mercy. A fist smashed into her stomach brutally, doubling her up. Her nose felt as if it suddenly burst into flames as Olga's knee came up to slam into it. Blinded and dazed Eeney came erect with blood rushing from her nose. Olga hit her, smashing a left to Eeney's face and knocking her into the ropes. Eeney was helpless and if Olga had been less vindictive the fight would have been over. Instead of trying to finish Eeney off the Russian girl smashed home blows to hurt her rather than knock her out.

Pain flooded over Eeney as the fists battered at her; she was helpless to do anything as the ropes rocked her into the blows. Then she felt herself falling and landed on the canvas. Her seconds were fast off the mark, crossing the ring to get to her, Olga was wild with rage, she tried to stamp on Eeney but was forced back by the seconds. She went to her corner and watched Eeney carried back to her own and laid on the stool. From the look of things Eeney would not be any more danger to her. Olga grinned savagely, hoping Eeney could come back to take more of a beating.

Mark Counter watched the two girls who were seconding Eeney. They did not appear to be doing much to help her. "Come on, Dutchy," he said and climbed on to the side of the ring.

Taking the cloth from one of the girls Mark dipped it into the water bucket she had brought with her. He wiped the blood from Eeney's face, she opened her eyes and looked at him, gasping for breath.

"Here, *liebchen*." Dutchy was by Mark's side and holding a glass of schnapps to her lips. "Drink some of this, it will give you strength."

Eeney sipped at the schnapps and coughed, gagging on the bite of it. Mark leaned closely and whispered some advice to her, she listened to him realising he knew what he was talking about.

For all of that Eeney did not appear to be in any shape to carry on the fight. Her eyes were half closed and she staggered weakly. Olga came to meet her with a smirk of delight on her face. This was going to be good; the German cow would wish she was never born.

Halting in front of Eeney the blonde reached out and shoved her head, tilting the chin back. Then Olga struck, her fist lashing up. To miss, Eeney's head jerked back allowing the fist to drive up in front of her face. Olga was wide open, stomach exposed to the brutal blow which Eeney swung with every ounce of her strength. The fist appeared to sink into Olga's plump stomach almost to the wrist. The blonde croaked in agony as she doubled over, her face an ashen grey green. She clutched at her stomach in agony, pain almost too much for her to bear knifing through her. The pain was short lived. Eeney's other fist came up, swinging with all the German girl had behind it. The smack of the blow sounded even above the cheers of the crowd. Olga's head snapped back, she came erect and over on to her back. The thud of her landing rocked the ring but she did not feel it. Olga was beyond feeling anything, and would be for some time to come.

There was no hope of Olga toeing the line at the end of the minute and Mundy, glowering at the exhausted Eeney announced her as winner and new champion. The crowd roared their approval. Dutchy ducked between the ropes and helped Eeney back to her corner, then he looked around for the gambler.

The other men were still at the table but the chair the gambler had occupied was empty; the man was gone.

CHAPTER NINE

Dutchy's Gain

Rage and impotence filled Dutchy as he looked at the empty seat. His money, the vital money for the mine was gone. He had made the bet without thinking of what it could mean if he lost. Now he was the winner and his dreams could be made real. The German girl was the reason he had won, she had taken a beating and come through for him. For what? He did not know, all he knew was his money was gone.

The gambler watched the fight at first without any worry for he knew the result was fixed in advance. Then as Eeney and Olga fought on he guessed something was wrong. He knew for certain when Bearcat Annie, just before the end of the fight went into her office.

Pushing his chair back the gambler rose and walked towards the door of the saloon. Every eye was on the fight and apart from a few yells for him to keep his head down he was not bothered. He reached the door and pushed it open as the yells of the crowd told him the fight was over. It was time he was far from there, hiding until things blew over. With this in mind he started to go through the doors and into the street. The night was dark out there and a fair crowd moved around. Once among them he would be safe.

A hand gripped the gambler's collar and dragged him backwards, something sharp pricking through his coat and to his spine. A voice, low, mocking and deadly came to his ears.

"You got a real poor sense of direction, friend. Dutchy's that ways."

The gambler was swung against the wall and found a slim, dark deadly-looking young man facing him. A man who held a razor sharp Bowie knife which said 'no' to any arguments. The gambler felt very scared; welshing on a bet was a serious thing in the rough frontier towns. The man who did it was lucky if he did not get hung by an irate crowd. That was why the Ysabel Kid took no chances when stopping the gambler and relieved him of the Derringer in his waistband.

The Ysabel Kid was as interested in the fight as any man in the saloon, but he was never the sort to allow his full attention to settle on one thing. He was alert and on the lookout for he knew Bearcat Annie did not like Dusty, whatever she said to the contrary. The Kid's Commanche blood gave him the primitive savage's ability to sense a person's real feelings. He knew they were in the country of the enemy and although he seemed to be at ease he was alert and watchful. He saw the gambler get up to leave and guessed what was planned, so unseen by the others he rose and followed.

"All right, back to Dutchy," the Kid said gently. "Move or I'll drop you where you stand." ·

The gambler turned and walked back towards the table

like a sick beagle coming to heel. He knew the Ysabel
Kid was not making an idle threat, he also knew the Kid
would be praised by any jury in the West for dropping
a welsher.

Dutchy was out of the ring by now, Dusty Fog and
his deputies on their feet, all knowing what had happened. There was anger in each pair of eyes and the
gambling man felt scared at the prospect of trouble.

"I'll have my money, please." Dutchy said, looking
relieved.

"I haven't enough to pay." The words came unwill-
ingly from the man.

"Send one of your pards to collect it from Bearcat
Annie," Dusty suggested. "You're one of the house's
men."

Clint Fang and several gunhung men started to move
in. "Never saw him afore," Fang stated.

"You said he was," Dutchy snapped.

"I mistook him for one of our men."

"You're a liar, Fang!"

Fang's face paled in sudden rage as he looked at the
small man who stood in front of him. To call a man a
liar in the West was just about the worst insult one could
manage. It was never employed unless the speaker was
full and ready to back that word with lead.

Talk in the saloon died away as with that instinct for
danger common to a Western crowd everyone in the
room realised something was wrong. All eyes were on
the group of men standing by the side of the ring. Eeney
Haufman, sitting on her stool, left there by the other
members of the troupe, looked down. She was lonely,
afraid and hurt, her body aching from the brutal fight.
Even the man who caused her to be fired was ignoring
her.

Dusty Fog watched Fang, knowing the man was going

to make a move this time. It was not Fang who was the danger in this situation but the men at his back. They might elect to fight and a crowded saloon was no place for a gun battle. Whatever play was made the innocent bystanders must not be placed in danger.

Down lashed Fang's hand toward his gun; he almost made it. Dusty Fog's left hand crossed in a sight-defying move, bringing the Army Colt up and lashing it across Fang's face knocking him backwards. Dusty followed the man up, his gun barrel smashing over and down on to Fang's head, pistol-whipping him to the ground. The move was done so fast that Fang's men were taken by surprise and none of them were set. Dusty's deputies were not expecting so sudden a move either; the difference was that two of them knew him. Mark and the Ysabel Kid saw the signs and knew just how Dusty would react. Consequently as soon as Dusty made his move they took action, guns coming out and covering Fang's backers.

"What's it all about, Marshal?" a miner asked.

"Dutchy made a bet with this man, now he can't pay off," Dusty answered and listened to the angry rumble from the crowd before going on. "He's a house man, or says he is."

The crowd were not at all unanimous in their idea of how to handle the gambler. Some were in favour of lynching, others, less harsh, wanted a coat of tar and feathers, others to ride the welshing gambler out of town on a rail. The gambler was aware he was due for one or other and panicked.

"I'm a house man," he howled, backing towards the lawmen. "Go ask Bearcat, she took me on."

"Where's Bearcat!" the shout went up.

Bearcat Annie listened to all the noise, sitting in her office and telling Mundy just what she thought of him;

that his engagement was cancelled and that he would not get paid for his trouble. She could guess what was going to happen and decided to leave the gambler to face the music. Then she thought of something. The man was no hero, he would talk if his skin was endangered. The crowd might not take any notice of him but she knew Dusty Fog would listen and investigate. That meant the young Texan would see Mundy and discover the result of the fight was rigged in advance. Dusty was also smart enough to add up two and two to get an answer like an attempt to stop Dutchy investigating his theory.

Getting to her feet she left the room, warning Mundy to stay where he was. She crossed the room, the crowd parting to allow her to pass. Halting at the group by the table, looking innocently at Dusty Fog, she asked, "What's the trouble?"

"Fang told us this *hombre* was a house gambler," Dusty answered, looking just as innocent. "So Dutchy laid down four thousand the German girl won the fight. Now the gambler says he can't pay and Fang allows he don't work here."

"Does he, Bearcat?" a man asked. "We don't want to rough up a man if it ain't needed. Is he one of your'n?"

"He works for me all right. But I said there wasn't to be any betting on the fight. He shouldn't have taken the money."

There was a growl of anger at this, the crowd knew the house gamblers were taking bets all the time the fight was in progress. Bearcat Annie listened to the rumble and read the signs right. If she did not call the play correctly she was going to have a riot on her hands.

"He wasn't working for me," she said, watching Dusty Fog all the time. "I reckon it'd make a right nice court case to decide who wins, Captain Fog."

"Yes'm." Dusty mentally raised his hat to the woman.

She knew the danger of a riot if she did not pay. She also knew his sense of duty would force him to prevent it. "It would. Only thing being I'll close your place until after we hear the ruling. And that might take time. Judge Shannon's a real busy man. It might take him a week or maybe even two before he gets around to making a judgment."

It was now Bearcat Annie's turn to raise a hat. Her idea would certainly hold Dutchy from getting his money. It would cost her far more for she knew Judge Shannon would follow whatever lead Dusty wanted to give in this matter. The Judge respected Dusty as a fair and impartial lawman. He would know Dusty was not acting for blind revenge in wanting the trial held up. Dusty was also well within his rights to say the saloon was closed. In a Western town a lawman could do pretty near what he wanted and no amount of legal skulldugery would affect his edict.

"All right." Bearcat Annie knew when she was licked and the time to holler calf rope was at hand. "I reckon I'm to blame for all this. I'll pay the bet off."

"Thank you, ma'am. I thought you'd play square."

Bearcat Annie met Dusty's eyes; there was a gleam of admiration in her gaze. If this young Texan would throw in with her and her boss they would take over the town. She knew there was no hope of that. Dusty Fog would never throw in with them. From now on it would be war to the death and the devil take the last man. The cheers of the crowd at her sporting offer to assume the loss were hollow mockery in her ears. The men in the crowd regarded her once more as a good sport, paying up for a loss which might not be her own fault. They did not know the bitter gall feeling which filled her. The plan so carefully laid was spoiled now. Worse, not only did Dutchy Schulze still have sufficient money to pay for his mining equipment he now possessed enough of her money to keep his mine going.

Dutchy was about to follow Bearcat Annie to the bar and collect his money when he saw Eeney sat on the stool in the ring, her head in her hands. He noticed the sobs which were shaking her frame and said, "Collect my winnings for me, please, Captain Fog."

"Sure, Dutchy."

Dutchy climbed into the ring, laying a hand on the girl's shoulder. In their own tongue he asked, "What is wrong?"

Eeney looked at him, her left eye was discoloured and her nose bloody. "It is nothing," she replied.

"Where are the others?" Dutchy looked around the empty ring. "Why did they leave you here?"

"Mundy says I have lost him money. I can no longer go with him."

Mark Counter swung into the ring. He did not speak German but did not need to. He had seen the way things were going, including Mundy leaving Eeney in the ring and knew what was wrong. "I'll get Doc to look her over down at the jail," he suggested. "Take her down there."

Dutchy helped the girl to her feet, Eeney hung on to him, feeling his strength as he put an arm around her. "Come, *liebchen*," he ordered.

Bearcat Annie handed Dusty Fog the money to pay off Dutchy, smiling with her lips but not her eyes. She saw Dutchy and Mark helping Eeney from the ring and her voice went over the noise of the crowd. "Hey, Dutchy, come on up and have a drink. Just to show there's no ill-feelings. Bring Eeney with you."

Dutchy was about to object, but all round were men he liked and was friendly with. They urged him and the girl towards the bar where drinks were waiting for them.

Eeney managed to raise a smile and answer the cheers of the crowd with a wave. "Great fight, gal," a miner whooped. "She'd give you a good whirl, Bearcat."

There was a hard gleam in Bearcat Annie's eyes as she looked at Eeney. With a smile on her lips she studied the girl. Bearcat Annie was known to be tough and a better than fair exponent of the art of hair-yanking, all-in frontier fighting as practised by the saloon women.

"She might at that. How about it, Eeney?"

"No!" Dutchy answered, his voice firm and definite. "From now on Eeney does not fight again."

"That's a real pity." Bearcat Annie held down her annoyance. If she could get this German girl in a fight she would have some of her revenge. "Reckon you're right. She doesn't want to get hurt after coming off lucky like that."

"What do you mean?" Eeney bristled like a cat; she was proud of her fighting skill. "Lucky?"

"Wasn't it luck that brought you through?" Bearcat Annie mocked. "I thought Russian Olga was whipping you."

The two women faced each other at the bar and the crowd felt a surge of anticipation running through it at the prospect of another fight. Dusty Fog looked the two women over and remarked, "One thing's for sure, Bearcat, you know when to make a challenge. You sit back and wait for an edge."

"Meaning?"

"Eeney's just ended a real tough fight, now you want her to stack against you. I call that being real brave."

The crowd listened to every word, the eagerness for the fight dying as they looked at the exhausted German girl, then at Bearcat Annie. The big blonde woman scowled. It appeared that Dusty Fog was once more stopping her plans. She wanted to fling herself at Eeney and savage the girl to relieve her own feelings. To do so now would lose her the favour of the crowd after regaining it by paying off the bet. Once more she forced through a smile. "All right. Pity you won't be staying here, girlie. Otherwise we might have put on a match."

Dutchy gently slipped the robe over Ecney's shoulders and with his arm around her turned from the bar. He did not mention it but if his plans went right Eeney would not be leaving town. However even if she stayed Dutchy did not intend to let her carry on making her living in the manner she had been doing it. Eeney was annoyed at Bearcat Annie's attitude, she felt ashamed by her refusal to meet the challenge. She started to strain away, to tell the fat blonde woman she was willing to go into the ring immediately.

"Come Eeney!" The voice was stern, and she felt herself obeying it meekly.

Bearcat Annie watched Dutchy and Eeney walking away and threw back her head. She laughed loud and bellowed, "Belly up to the bar, boys. Looks like the champion's retired."

There was a laugh at that and Eeney, face flushing scarlet tried to turn. Dutchy kept hold of her shoulder, meeting her eyes and saying gently, "No, *liebchen,* you have finished with that way now."

Dusty and his deputies followed Dutchy from the saloon. The small Texan looked at the robe Eeney wore and asked, "Where are your clothes, ma'am?"

"At the back of the saloon, in Mundy's wagon. He said I could not have them."

"Did huh?" Dusty's reply was mild. "Reckon he can be talked round if you do it right. Let's go, Lon."

Eeney was about to say something but she was too late, Dusty and the Ysabel Kid were gone, walking around the corner of the saloon. Mark looked at the girl then at Dutchy. "Come on. Let's go down to the jail and wait."

"Mundy won't give up my clothes," Eeney warned. "He is very violent when annoyed and he carries a gun."

"Don't you worry none, ma'am. Ole Dusty's real persuasive when he needs to be," Mark answered. "Come on, let's get off the streets."

The back of the saloon was surrounded by a board fence and used as a dump for cases of empty bottles. A street ran behind the saloon and on it stood Mundy's wagon, lit by a lamp. Inside the four girls were sitting at the back, Olga lay on a rough bunk, still unconscious and Mundy was trying to open a trunk.

"Don't bother, friend. We can carry it without emptying her."

Turning Mundy saw two men, one tall, the other smaller. They stood in the light of the lamp, the badges on their vests reflecting the light. "What do you want here?" he growled.

"Miss Haufman's gear," Dusty answered. "So turn her loose and we'll herd her to home."

Mundy straightened up, his lips drawing back in a sneer. "Yeah?" he asked, his hand dropping casually to his coat pocket.

"Yeah!" Dusty's right hand made a sight-defying move, the left side Colt coming out and lined. "Just hand her over, right now."

Slowly Mundy's eyes went from the gun to Dusty's face. He could read no sign of indecision or lack of purpose in that face. He knew that if he did not hand over the box he would wish he had. "This's it. I was just going to take the money she's made me lose."

Dusty climbed into the wagon and shoved the box towards the Kid. He holstered his gun and turned to face

Mundy. "I don't like you or your way of making a living, *hombre*," he warned. "You set that fight up to cost a friend of mine plenty."

"You can't prove that," Mundy sneered.

Two hands bunched his coat lapels and dragged him forward, cold grey eyes on his face from real close. The voice which replied to him was not loud yet it was a voice he never forgot.

"Mister, I don't aim to prove it. Dutchy came out the winner and I'm satisfied. You'll be out of this town by noon tomorrow. If you're not I'll send you on your way personally."

With a contemptuous thrust of his powerful arms, Dusty sent the man staggering back. Dusty saw the girls moving to allow their boss as painful a landing as possible and knew they did not care for him. Turning, Dusty was about to leave the wagon when he saw the Ysabel Kid point like a coon-hound hitting a hot scent. The box fell from his hands, his right twisting to bring the old Dragoon out. Dusty swung back, expecting Mundy to be making some treacherous move, his left hand bringing out its gun. The man still lay where he had landed and made no move which might have caused this sudden action by the Ysabel Kid.

"All right. Come on out with your hands showing!"

Dusty turned and swung from the wagon as he heard the Kid give out with his challenge while lining his gun on the shadows formed by the high fence. Landing by his friend's side he tried to see what attracted the other but could not. For a moment he thought for once the Kid was wrong. "I'm counting to three, then shooting," the Kid went on. "One!"

Something moved in the blackness, something which the Kid's Indian keen senses located. The two young

Texans were tense ready to either shoot or hit the ground. Into the light came a tall, thin shape clad in a black suit and a high hat.

"Howdy, Mr. Grimwood," Dusty greeted, recognising the undertaker. "You like to scare the Kid out of a year's growth?"

"It sure did," agreed the Kid, surprised that the undertaker had managed to come so close before being detected by his exceptionally keen ears. "You're a mite off your home range, Mr. Grimwood."

Grimwood gulped, his face holding a look like a man caught out doing something he should not. He glanced back in the direction he had just come, to where the red lamp of Jenny's place gleamed in the darkness.

"I was merely taking a walk, marshal."

Dusty holstered his gun, a grin playing around his lips. Grimwood was loud in his condemnation of the red light section of town and a stout member of the Civic Improvement Guild. From the guilty look on his face he was doing something he should not. "Bad area for a man to be walking, back here."

"I agree. I agree." Grimwood looked around again. "Could I speak to you alone Captain Fog?"

"Why sure. Lon, take the box down to the jail."

The Ysabel Kid winked as he holstered his gun and took up the box. He could make a fair guess at where Grimwood's walk took him. He turned and headed for the jail. Grimwood watched him go and with the nervous, mother-hen attitude of a man caught doing something really wrong.

They went into the alley at the side of the saloon and Grimwood halted, his sallow face working nervously. "Er, I . . . er . . . that is. Well, it's like this, Captain Fog. I was merely taking a walk along the street there. I have a toothache and er . . ."

"I understand, Mr. Grimwood." Dusty's tone showed that he *did* understand all too well.

"Of course you're a man of the world, Captain. You realise what the consequences of my walk would mean if the wrong people heard of it. After all I'm a founder member of the Civic Improvement Guild and . . . well . . . cr. I . . ."

Once more Grimwood floundered to a stop. He was obviously embarrassed and Dusty could guess why. Grimwood was one of those pious-talking do-gooding kind of hypocrites who believe that the common folk must be protected from lust and sin while being quite ready to dabble in that same lust and sin on the sly. It fitted in with the impression Dusty formed of Grimwood on the few times he had met the undertaker.

"Like I said, I understand."

"There are some who would not take a charitable view of my walk. Especially as I have the misfortune to be coming from this direction. May I rely on your discretion, Captain Fog?"

"Why sure." Dusty ignored the folded bill Grimwood held to him. "It's none of my business where you spend your time. Goodnight, Mr. Grimwood."

Dusty walked away and Grimwood left the alley to go back in the direction of his shop. The young marshal was still smiling when he entered the jail office and found all his deputies sat around describing the fight to the Bollingers who had been acting as jailers while the lawmen took a rest. Maggie was looking Eeney over as the German girl sat talking with Dutchy. The big woman nodded a greeting to Dusty and remarked, "We're going to have a wedding soon."

"What do you mean?" Dusty asked.

"Dutchy and Eeney. He told us as soon as they came in. She looked some surprised but she hasn't objected."

Dutchy was oblivious of everything except for Eeney. He looked down at her and told her of his plans. She was silent and thoughtful, wondering how she had come to be mixed up in this. For some time she had been wanting to leave the troupe but knew she could not make a living if she did. Now she was being given that chance. Dutchy talked eagerly and in German, speaking as only a man can when using his native tongue and to a woman he loved. Yet he did not speak of love, only of his plans. The money won that night would pay for the mining equipment outright and still leave enough for them to pay help and make a home. He wanted to buy her a big house but she refused that offer, asking only that she be able to stay with him.

Finally he rose and came to where Dusty was seated filling in the Marshal's log on the desk. "Captain, I am to marry Eeney in the morning. We would take it as a great honour if you would be the best man."

"Sure thing, Dutchy. One thing though. Miss Haufman's going to stay with Maggie here tonight and you're stopping in the backroom. Then tomorrow your money's going back into the bank."

"I agree, Captain. But is it necessary for your men to guard us?"

"More than ever now."

The deputies went out to make their rounds of the town and Maggie took Eeney out back to wash up. Dusty carried on writing up his log, the daily record of all that happened to his men. He was just finishing when Maggie came back. "Eeney's in your place, changing. Say, was she really fighting in there?"

"Dutchy didn't hand her that black eye to make her accept him," Dusty replied with a grin.

"Women fist fighters, what'll they think of next?" Maggie snorted then gave a smile. "Lon told us you caught old Buzzard going to see his girl friend. I've seen him at it before now."

"What, visiting Jenny's?"

"No Bearcat Annie's place. I've seen him sneak in the back there more than once."

CHAPTER TEN

He's A Calhoun

Dusty sat looking at Maggie Bollinger for a time. "Bearcat Annie's place?" he asked finally.

"Sure. I've seen him going in the back way at night more than once. Not that he's the only one. I've seen some more going in there who'd be real shocked if they thought they'd been seen."

Dusty was a suspicious young man; he looked for motives beyond the first and most obvious to meet the eye. The woman's words took him by surprise; he had been sure from Grimwood's actions that the undertaker was coming from Jenny's house. The very way Grimwood acted was enough to make him believe that. Yet it appeared he was wrong, Grimwood was going to Bearcat Annie's saloon for some reason. There was a solution to it. Grimwood might have been at Jenny's, making a change from his usual haunt. That he was using the back way into the saloon did not surprise Dusty. Grimwood

and those other men Maggie Bollinger mentioned were
the sort who would be horrified at the thought of being
seen entering a place of sin. Grimwood's actions were
in keeping with his pious, hypocritical way of life. Even
that furtive, false friendship was what Dusty could expect, so was the discussion as between two men of the
world. There was a reason behind Grimwood's desire
that Dusty think he had been to Jenny's place. It was a
kind of cover; he could always claim, truthfully, that he
had never been in Jenny's place if the young Texan was
indiscreet enough to talk.

"You and Cy take Eeney home with you, Maggie,"
he said. "And don't let her out of your sight. She's not
to go with anyone, no matter what they tell her. If I send
for her I'll send one of the boys. Don't under any cir-
cumstances let Eeney go with anybody else."

"Sure, Cap'n. Do you think that fat blonde cow'd try
to get her own back on Eeney for winning the fight?"

"She might at that," Dusty answered. He did not want
to bother Maggie with his ideas that there was some
more sinister motive behind any attempt which might be
made.

Eeney went with Maggie and her husband, and
Dutchy, and following them, one on either side of the
street, went Doc Leroy and Rusty Willis.

The next morning Dusty Fog was best man at the
wedding, but the honeymoon was postponed until some
later and safer date.

Dusty left the wedding breakfast before the others and
returned to the jail. Matt Gillem was waiting. The old
banker greeted Dusty but there was a worried look in his
eyes.

"There's trouble, boy," he said.

Dusty was not unduly worried by this. Since taking
over as Marshal he found Matt Gillem to be very co-

operative. Neither he nor the rest of the Town Council interfered in the way Dusty handled things, just sitting back and watching the results come in. However, with Quiet Town becoming tamer there were people who asked why so large a police force was required.

"It's the Civic Improvement Guild. They want you to close the red light houses down," Gillem explained. "You know how the Council stands on it and we leave you to make your own decision."

"It's made. The miners need some place to go."

"There's some talk about you getting paid off by the owners." Gillem went on, watching the anger in Dusty's eyes. "Look, son. I know there's nothing in it. You know what some of them lot are like when they get stopped doing what they want."

"I know." Dusty's voice was grim and cold.

"I talked with the editor of the Quiet Town Gazette. He's got an editorial demanding investigation of the local law. Wants all your records and log producing."

"It's there!" Dusty indicated the desk. "My badge is with it if they want that too."

"They might, boy. *We* don't. See, we know that you're acting for the best and I've come out flatfooted to say we back you to the hilt."

Dusty smiled, looking young and innocent again. He knew it took a lot of courage for the City Fathers to go against the opinion of the influential minority of the Civic Improvement Guild. It gave him a feeling of pride that they would do so for him.

The editorial caused some comment when it appeared. Most of the comment was adverse, for people remembered how their town had been only a few short weeks before. Through the town, from the storekeepers who could now run their businesses in peace to the miners who had been given Dusty Fog's treatment for the hangover, all were of one mind. Dusty Fog was the finest town marshal to wear the badge in Quiet Town, they wanted him there and would resist stoutly any attempt to dethrone him.

The Gazette editor was no fool. He could read the signs and brought out a second edition for the first time in the history of his paper. The editorial in this was far more complimentary to Dusty Fog, pointing out how well he handled the town and insisting that he be allowed to continue without unwarranted interference.

So matters stood and four days went by. On the early afternoon of the fifth Bearcat Annie entered her private office and found she had a visitor. He sat at the desk, a bottle of whisky in front of him and a glass by his hand. His eyes cold as he looked at her.

"Well?" the man asked, his voice hard.

"Well?" she countered, for she knew this man who ruled her very well. He was in a temper and there was danger for Bearcat Annie who was his second in command and much closer than that.

"The Texans are still in town. Schulze still has his money. We are no nearer to achieving our end than we were at first."

"I know. Think I haven't been worrying over it. I wanted to use my boys to stick Dutchy up but you wouldn't have it. You turned Calhoun and his loboes out and they made a mess of it."

"We made a fatal mistake," the man answered. "We underestimated Dusty Fog. I thought he was just a fast gun, hired to kill off the bad hats, like Hickok would do. But I know I was wrong now. I used Calhoun's bunch because I know he is no fool. They aren't known in town, your men are. It'd be real smart to send Fang and his crew out to take Dutchy Schulze and have somebody recognise them."

Bearcat Annie knew this without being told. "It wasn't my fault we missed getting his money when he bet on the fight. That lousy German cow won when she was told to lose. One of these days I'll get her and tear every damned hair out of her head."

"You'll do no such thing!" The man's eyes glowed cold fire. "I've told you before blind revenge is stupid. You played that game in the saloon all wrong. I heard how you tried to make her fight you. Listen, you're not dealing with one of these fast gun morons where Dusty Fog is concerned. He's a thinking man, he doesn't just look at things as they appear. He knows why you wanted to work the girl over. If she meets up with any accident you're the one he'll be looking for. You'll leave her be. Act friendly to her if you meet her in the street from now on. She's married to Schulze now and done with the fighting game. You leave her be."

"All right," Bearcat Annie sounded sullen.

The man's hand shot out, gripping her wrist with a strength that was out of all proportion to his appearance. "Make sure it is!" The voice was low and vibrant. "We're playing for big stakes here."

"Why don't we take what we've got and clear out?" Bearcat Annie asked. "We're holding enough to make it worth our while."

"That's what's wrong with you, Annie. You think small, like a saloon slut. I wonder how I ever got myself tied in with you. I'm not thinking of a few thousand dollars. I'm thinking of a fortune beyond your avaricious little dreams. A mining empire. You know I got my own surveyor into the mine and he gave me the same report Schulze brought out. There is a rich vein under the bedrock and so far the miners don't know about it. They've never seen such a thing and are not willing to listen to Schulze. When that vein peters out the mines will be closed. We can buy them for a song. But only if Schulze doesn't get his chance to prove his idea."

"You could always wipe Roxie Delue out."

"I thought of that but Calhoun's lost men and we haven't managed to bring any more in to fill the gap. I thought downing old man Delue would stop the last freight outfit but she's stayed on."

From the outside door came a knock. The change in the man was instant and decisive. He kicked back the chair, coming to his feet with his hand sliding under his coat to bring out a Colt Wells Fargo revolver. Backing across to the door of a cupboard he opened it and stepped inside. Cut into the woodwork and disguised by the decorative scroll were two eye holes which gave Bearcat Annie's mysterious visitor a clear view of everything which went off in the room. The thinness of the wood allowed him to hear every word said; it was a very useful arrangement, allowing a man who wished to stay in the background of things to hear and see all that went on.

Bearcat Annie waited until the cupboard door closed, then she went across the room and opened the other door. A smallish man entered, a man wearing old range clothes. He was a wizened, quick looking man, his face seamed and scarred, yet with the shrewd cunning of a weasel about it. On his head was a battered black hat which looked as if it was often slept on. Low at each side hung a Navy Colt, the cleanest things about him.

"What're you doing here?" Bearcat Annie asked. "You shouldn't be walking the streets by daylight, Calhoun."

Bronco Calhoun slipped into the room like a wolf coming up to a poisoned bait. His keen eyes took in everything, including a small bottle which lay on the floor, dropped by Annie's previous visitor. His nostrils quivered like an animal's as he went to the desk.

"Likker's all gone, gal. You alone in here?"

"You're expecting me maybe to be entertaining Dusty Fog?"

"Naw. Just thought I heard you talking to somebody when I come to the door. Didn't sound like you was talking to one of your hired men. More like you was getting telled something by your boss."

"Boss?" Bearcat Annie frowned. "You know I'm the boss. I told you that when you first came in here."

Bronco Calhoun grinned, his wolf sharp face showing mocking disbelief. "You told all right, gal. I got to thinking, maybe you ain't the big boss. Ramrod, mebbee, but not the big augur hisself. Good fight you put on in there. Like to see me another. Thought you and that German gal were going to tangle. I'd have bet on her."

"Get your drink and go back to the hideout, Calhoun," Bearcat Annie's voice was brittle now.

"Never been in the backroom here afore. Classy place, ain't it. Good big cupboards. A man could hide hisself in one of them easy. Tell him to come on out, gal."

Bearcat Annie's hand dropped towards the desk in a casual move. With a snarl Calhoun brought out his right hand gun, lining on her. She stood still and the gun barrel swung towards the cupboard door. "Come on out, friend. I reckon I can hit you afore you hit me."

The door swung open and the man stood exposed, his gun lined on Calhoun. "I don't think you can."

"Waal, I swan. So you're the big augur. I never believed Annie when she said she was blackmailing you into hiding us out. Never thought you was the big wheel though."

The man eyed Calhoun mockingly. "Didn't you?"

"Naw, didn't even think the gal was the big augur. She ain't smart enough for that."

"Easy now!" The other man's voice was hard. "That's

my wife you're talking about. You've been told to keep off the streets."

"I been told a whole lot of things since I come here. Like how I should work with rebs and how we was going to make money. All I've done so far is lose sons."

"We didn't tell Bert to try that game with Dusty Fog," Bearcat Annie pointed out. "You can't blame us for it going wrong."

"I don't. It's that damned button who cut in and spoiled the play I want. Who was he?"

"Army scout called Happy Day. Works for Roxie Delue now," Annie supplied the information. "Why didn't Deke cut in before Counter drew?"

"Bert allowed he could handle it. He called the play. Wouldn't want a Calhoun to be accused of being yeller." Bronco Calhoun was sincere in that. Bad though he was and there were few who could equal him in out and out cruel evil, he lived by a certain code. His sons were brought up to it and proud of their name. That was what saved Mark Counter from backshooting lead when he faced Bert Calhoun. "Me'n the boys are getting tired of hanging on here. We've got some money to spend and we're only waiting to take the bank afore we leave."

"Why don't you try it?" Bearcat Annie's husband asked.

"You know why. Them shotgun guards. They'd cut us to pieces before we could make a move. If they wasn't there——."

Bronco Calhoun's words were stopped by a knock on the saloon door. The other man jerked his head towards the cupboard and followed Calhoun inside, closing the door. Bearcat Annie looked around to make sure nothing was on view to give her caller the idea she had been entertaining. The knock came again as she swept the whisky glass into the desk drawer and opened the door.

Clint Fang stood there, trying to see into the room.

"What do you want, Fang?"

"You got callers, Bearcat?" he answered, moving forward.

"No, come right in." She stood aside, allowing him to enter and watched him looking around with curiosity plain on his face. "What's wrong?"

"Nothing much. Roxie Delue's back in town. Her and that Happy Day's gone to the jail."

"That supposed to interest me."

"I don't know." Fang still was not sure that Bearcat Annie was alone. He knew better than press the point. "It might. There's a drifter in the bar. He recognised Happy Day from some place or other."

"So?"

"Come as a bit of a surprise to me when he told me. Couldn't believe it at first, but he says it's true."

"What's true?" Bearcat Annie was getting annoyed at the mystery Fang was building and the way he looked around her office.

"Who Happy Day is. He reckons Day's name's Calhoun. He's one of Bronco's boys."

Bearcat Annie did not reply immediately. She tried to think of what her husband would want making of this. If the boy was one of Bronco Calhoun's sons it could mean Dusty Fog knew of it and was working in with Bronco to doublecross them. She doubted it, or that the man was even one of Calhoun's boys.

"All right, Fang. Go and keep him in here. Let him drink free if he's broke."

Fang did not like the idea of leaving when he was almost sure the mysterious leader and boss of Bearcat Annie's was hidden in the cupboard. He knew the tone the woman used, it was one which gave him pause. The man hidden in the cupboard obviously did not want to be seen. If so he would take precautions not to be. Those same precautions could consist of a bullet into anyone who tried to pierce his cloak of mystery. So with this thought in mind Fang turned on his heel and walked from the room, hearing the lock click behind him. He crossed to the bar where a man dressed in buckskins leaned, drinking.

The cupboard door opened and the two men stepped out. "Fang's getting too nosey, Annie."

"I've thought that for a spell now," she replied, watching her husband for some sign of what he aimed to do about the new development. "Is it one of your boys, Bronco?"

"Naw. All my boys are with me." Bronco Calhoun could barely remember the boy he had left for dead all those years before. "Must be some fool kid trying to build a rep for hisself."

"Be a dangerous thing to do in a town like this," Bearcat Annie's husband put in. "Folks wouldn't take to having a Calhoun here in town. They might even want to lynch him."

"He's at the jail. Dusty Fog'll try and stop them doing it," Bearcat Annie pointed out.

"That's right. Him against the town," her husband agreed. "He's good with a gun, so are his men. But they can't handle the whole town. They'll need help and I don't reckon Matt Gillem'll stand by and see them go wanting. He'll pull his guards from the bank and—."

"Me'n my boys'll move in to take it."

"Bringing the money back to the hideout to share."

"Sure thing, friend," Calhoun lied. "What do you reckon I am, dishonest?"

Calhoun did not intend to bring the money back at all. He was tired of being in Quiet Town for the place was no longer flowing with milk and honey. When he

took the bank he and his men would keep right on going.
He knew that. So did the other man. Bearcat Annie's
husband knew he was to be doublecrossed but did not
mind. The money in the bank was not vital to his plans
and none of his own wealth, save a small deposit was
in the bank. The bulk of his, and his wife's not incon-
siderable gains, were safely locked in his well-hidden
safe. The title deeds of the businesses they owned, the
freight companies they had bought from scared-off owners and other incriminating evidence was in the big safe
at the side of the room in which they now stood. It was
an ideal arrangement. Apart from Bearcat Annie there
was, as far as he knew, nothing to connect him with the
crime empire he had built in Quiet Town. Bearcat Annie
would not talk and a wife could not give evidence against
her husband even if she wanted to. Whatever happened
he was safe, there was nothing wrong with his plans.
Nothing except a sheet of paper he had long forgotten
which now lay gathering dust at the bottom of the safe.
That sheet of paper was enough to stretch his neck yet
neither he, or Bearcat Annie remembered it.

"You'd better get your boys ready," the man told
Calhoun. "It'll take a mite of stirring to get a mob going.
I reckon just before dark everything will be set. I'll get
it going as soon as I can. Annie, go keep Fang busy. If
he sees me I'll have to kill him and we still need him."

Bearcat Annie walked from her office. Fang saw her
appear and turned to make for the door, but her shout
stopped him. He turned and walked back, looking annoyed at his failure to see who was the power behind
Bearcat Annie.

"You keep that feller here?" she asked.

"Sure. He's at the bar. What do you want doing?"

"Get around town. Spread word about that Happy

Day being one of the Calhouns. Stir up a lynch mob and get them to the jail."

Fang hesitated; he wanted badly to get a chance to see who Bearcat Annie's boss was. "How about that feller?"

"We'll keep him here to tell the mob that Happy Day's really a Calhoun. Get going, Fang. Take as many men as you need." Bearcat Annie turned to go back to her office when a thought struck her. "Fang, hire me some good guns and send them here. If Dusty Fog stops that mob he's going to come looking for me. One way or another I'm going to break him, or he'll break me."

Bearcat Annie returned to her office, knowing Fang was seething with unasked questions. He was becoming too much of a menace. Early in their acquaintance he had tried using his charm on her and learned the hard way she was not to be had like a common calico cat from the dancehalls. From then on their relationship was once more of employee and employer. Then he started to grow increasingly suspicious and to ask questions. Bearcat Annie hoped Dusty Fog would find time to kill Fang, it would save her the necessity of having it done.

She glanced around the room, checking that everything was all right. One good thing about her husband was that he was rarely panicked into making a mistake. He never left anything to chance. Then she saw the bottle laying by the chair he had sat in. A startled curse came from her as she went to pick it up. That was what gave Bronco Calhoun his warning she was not alone. If Fang had seen it he would know who her visitor was for there was only one man in the town who would have such a bottle.

Picking the bottle up she took the keys to the safe from her desk and opened the iron door. Glancing in as she tossed the bottle on to the papers she found herself for the first time realising the implications of the contents of the safe. If there was anything went wrong she would be the one who the blame fell on. It made her think as she went to the door of her office after locking the safe and returning the keys to the desk drawer.

In the saloon a rumble of talk was going round. Two of her prettiest girls were keeping the buckskin clad stranger occupied and distracting his interest from the angry crowd being worked up by a couple of Bearcat Annie's men. The big blonde woman crossed the room and listened.

"I tell you, boys," a gambler was saying to the angry-looking crowd who were all round him. "There's one of them Calhouns in town. He's at the jail now and the marshal's protecting him. Are we going to stand for that?"

The yell of "No!" was loud and from outside could be heard a deep roar of other men being worked up to fury pitch.

"All right then," the gambler yelled. "Let's go and get that Calhoun, then hang him from a tree."

CHAPTER ELEVEN

Lynch Mob

There was a happy group in the Marshal's office as Roxie Delue and her now inseparable companion, Happy Day announced they were ready to leave for Newton and bring back the mining equipment for Dutchy. They and the deputies of the police force were all happy although Roxie was annoyed at missing Dutchy's wedding. Dusty Fog sat watching them all, a smile on his face. Yet he was worried for Doc and Rusty were planning to head out down to Newton themselves to find their boss and the rest of their outfit. That was going to leave the Quiet Town police force short of men but it was far from being as serious as it would have when they first arrived. He could not blame Doc and Rusty. They were cowhands first and lawmen second. He knew the loyalty every cowhand felt to his brand and knew they wanted to get back to the Wedge.

The door of the office was thrown open and Irish Pat

came in. "Cap'n Fog!" he said. "There's trouble. Word's got out you've got a Calhoun down here and a mob's stirring up."

Dusty glanced at Happy Day and Roxie gave a startled cry. She clutched the buckskin shirt, looking at Happy with scared eyes. The small Texan went to one of the side windows and looked out. Men were coming from saloons in ugly groups, shouting to each other. All to well he knew how a lynch mob could start. Men's feelings ran high and with the aid of raw frontier whisky passions were soon inflamed to danger peak. The word would be rolling like a prairie grass fire, leaping from saloon to saloon, bringing more enraged men out. The miners had little or no love for the name of Calhoun, remembering friends killed and gold shipments stolen. There were others who were not interested in revenge, but would go along with the mob merely to be in any trouble that was going.

Dusty swung from the window, his deputies standing alert and ready for action, just waiting for his orders to them. His eyes ran around them. Dutchy, Eeney, Cy and Maggie Bollinger all watched him in some surprise.

"You ain't got no Calhoun in jail, Cap'n," Maggie remarked.

It was Happy Day who spoke. "They want me."

"You?" Maggie's eyes narrowed.

"My name's Calhoun."

"But he's not one of the Calhoun gang!" Roxie was grim and defiant, standing by Happy's side.

Maggie studied the girl for a moment, then looked at Dusty Fog. She knew the young Texan was aware of Happy Day's identity and that was good enough for her. She and her husband knew Dusty too well to think he would side with anyone who was not all right. If he was satisfied with Happy Day so were they.

"What do you want me to do, Cap'n?" she asked and went to hug Roxie. "Don't you worry none, gal. The Cap'n'll see you through."

Dusty was watching the mob growing, down on the square, men steering clear of the jail, going round the back of the opposite buildings to join the fast-growing mob in front of Bearcat Annie's place. Then they started forward, coming towards the jail, the ugly rumble of the mob-cry sounding louder all the time. The small Texan knew he didn't have much time to do anything at all, his mind was working fast.

"Cy, take scatterguns, you and Dutchy, cover the back of the jail. Don't let anybody get in. Mark, Lon, Doc, Rusty. We're going on to the porch and try to talk some sense into that bunch there. You ladies stay here."

"How about me?"

Dusty turned to look at Happy Day. The young man was grim-faced and determined looking. There was something in Happy's eyes which made Dusty reply, "You're coming out there with us. We've got to stop them and you might help."

The mob was nearing now, filling the street. Dusty jerked his head to the door. Mark Counter was first out, the Ysabel Kid following him, then Doc and Rusty moving to the other side of the door. Dusty came next, closing the door behind him and looking down at the approaching men.

"That's near enough!"

The words were not spoken loud and Dusty did not draw his guns. Yet the mob surged to a halt. It was a hard crowd, fighting men and all of them armed yet they came to a halt at the words of the small, soft-talking Texan. Every man in this crowd knew the way Dusty Fog and his men could draw and shoot. They knew that there stood a group who were the peer of any in town.

"We want that Calhoun, Cap'n," a miner shouted and there was a yell of agreement to it.

"Which Calhoun is that?" Dusty answered.

"Don't try and fool us. We know Happy Day is and we want him."

"You won't get him," Dusty answered and the crowd surged forward slightly.

"Ease back there, all of you. Happy, come on out."

Happy Day stepped from the office with Roxie Delue behind him, the girl pale yet facing the angry snarls of the crowd without shrinking. The mob roared out in anger as they saw Happy but the forward surge halted before those unflinching Texas men.

In the crowd, on the other side of the street Fang watched and tried to stir up the mob to take action. "Get him. Stretch his neck."

Again came the mob roar and the crowd surged forward but the ones in front, those who would first face the guns of the Texans still held back. Dusty watched every move, not drawing his guns or making any hostile move. There was something in those grey eyes to give pause to the boldest. He was the law, they knew it, every man here. The crowd were acting with typical mob psychology. To their minds they were acting for the law and the defenders of the rights of the citizen. If they hung the Calhoun man they would be acting in the interests of justice. Yet by some strange quirk the lynch mob would not open fire either on Happy or the lawmen who guarded him. To do so would not be according to the law and they felt they would then no longer be defenders of the right.

"We want Calhoun!" a man yelled.

"Get them all, they're in cahoots!" Fang roared. "Get them all."

Dusty could see who was shouting and knew there

was a slight chance to handle the affair without killing. He knew that the quickest way to handle a mob was to get the leaders, the men who were doing all the talking.

"You talk real big for a man in a crowd, *hombre*!" he called. "Hiding behind folks and shouting. Makes you a real big man."

"Come on out, Fang." The Ysabel Kid also knew who was talking. "Don't try to use a mob to do what you never could."

"They're hunting time, boys!" Fang yelled back. "Rush 'em, they won't shoot."

Dusty knew they were all sitting on a keg of gunpowder with the fuse lit and running out. The mob was holding back right now but it could leap forward if prodded the wrong way and working up enough hatred into its collective system. The men here were for the most part honest enough and at other times would have been willing to back Dusty. Right now they were stirred with hatred for the Calhouns and nothing more mattered to them. He also knew that if he showed any weakness all was lost.

"Look, boys. There'll be no lynching here. For one thing Happy isn't one of the gang. For another, nobody's going to lynch any man in my town. If you try there will be shooting. And for what? You're being used by a yeller rat who wants to get back at me and hasn't the guts to do it himself."

"Don't listen to him!" Fang yelled, still in the back of the crowd.

"Listen to the brave man!" Dusty's voice lashed at the crowd. "Just listen to him. Hiding among you, doesn't dare show his-self. That's the man you're backing. That's the man you're following."

It was a good try and for a moment Dusty thought it would succeed. The crowd were wavering, the more sober starting to ask each other just what they were doing there. Fang saw the wavering and took a chance. He was a professional gambler, which meant he was a student of men. He had studied Dusty Fog and knew things about the small Texan.

Moving back to the far side of the street Fang gripped the hitching rail and hauled himself up to stand on it. "Here I am!" he yelled, making sure his hands were well clear of his guns. "Standing here where you can see me. I'm saying we should take that damned Calhoun son and string him up along with those Texans who're working in cahoots with him."

Dusty could have cursed when he saw the way Fang called his bluff. He knew, as Fang knew, that he would not, could not shoot the gambler down. The moment Dusty or any of his men started to shoot the crowd would fight back. True the young Texans were masters of the gun-fighting trade and could do great destruction before they were cut down. But they would be cut down. No six men could stand up to and live through the concentrated hell of lead which that mob could pour out at them. Besides, as a lawman, Dusty could not deliberately open fire on men whose only crime was folly and misguided sense of justice.

"I'll fetch him off there like a coon from a log," said the Ysabel Kid from the corner of his mouth, holding his voice down.

"No go, Lon," Dusty snapped back. He knew the dark young man was no moralist and quite ready to shoot Fang from the rail without worrying about such a small technicality as the gambler being unarmed. Dusty also knew that to do so would make Fang a martyr and bring about the shooting he wished to avoid.

The men on the porch stood grim-faced, attention on the crowd, yet all waiting for whatever play Dusty called.

By Happy Day's side, grim-faced as the men, yet wishing she was wearing her usual clothes and gunbelt instead of a gingham dress, Roxie Delue looked down. She knew most of the crowd, yet she also knew they would never listen to reason, even from her. It was enough to make a girl want to sob. In the days they had been together Happy had told her of his life with Bronco Calhoun and she pitied him while admiring the guts which kept him honest.

Fang, still standing on the rail, knew his hand took the pot. He had called the bluff and come out the winner. The Texans would not risk shooting him, they would not open the shooting. The mob would follow him now. "Get that Calhoun son, boys!" he roared. "If them Texans try to stop you, kill 'em!"

Matt Gillem sat in the back office of the bank engaged in no more bankerly occupation than playing solitaire. He could hear the noise down town and was on the verge of investigating when there was a knock on the door and Kennet entered. The young bank manager looked worried and said, "Grimwood's just come to tell you a lynchmob is at the jail. They've got an idea Captain Fog is holding one of the Calhoun gang and they're trying to get him."

Gillem came to his feet, a low curse breaking from his lips. He had seen lynch mobs before and so far it was a curse Quiet Town was free from. All too well he knew Dusty Fog would never allow any prisoner to be lynched or taken from him. He also knew no five men could stand up to a mob. There was only one thing a man could do in a case like that. Opening his desk drawer he took out a Dragoon Colt, checked the nipples to ensure all were capped, then thrusting the heavy old gun into his waistband snapped, "Get the guards for me."

For an instant Kennet stood and appeared to be going

to object. The three shotgun-armed guards were a precaution he approved of. To take them away would mean that for the first time since the town boomed open the bank would be unguarded. It only took him that instant to realise that the three men might help to turn the tide in favour of law and order. Captain Fog and his men had worked hard to bring Quiet Town to some semblance of peace and order. They needed help now and the bank was one place which would be able to give it. Turning on his heel Kennet walked from the room and Matt Gillem followed, calling the men down from the verandah.

Bearcat Annie looked around her partially deserted saloon. Only the men Fang sent along were there and the man who had recognised Happy Day. He was still talking to the dance-hall girls, only eight or so of whom remained. Looking up he saw how the saloon was emptied of customers and became aware of the sounds in the street. "Say, what's going on?" he asked.

"Why, they're going to lynch that awful ole Calhoun boy you recognised," one of the girls replied.

"What?" The man came to his feet, his face scored and angry. "Why those stupid fools. I've got to—."

"Set easy, friend," a man ordered, moving from the bar, gun in hand.

"Set nothing!" the buckskin dressed man growled. "I've got to get out there and stop them—."

"Stop nothing. The boys want their fun."

Three tall Texas men who had come into the saloon shortly after the lynch mob looked at each other. One of their number nodded his head, his scarred face showing no expression. The three turned and walked from the saloon to join two others of their kind who were sitting on cow-horses by the side of a chuckwagon driven by a short, whiskery and leathery-looking old timer. The scarred young man went to a big bay horse and swung into the saddle with an easy grace. He jerked his head and the other men started their horses forward.

The crowd around the jail rumbled out their indecision. They were all beginning to see that there would be far more to taking the prisoner from Dusty Fog than they first expected. The crowd half expected the town law to hand over Happy Day without any argument. Now they were seeing that the only way to take him would be by fighting. Not one man in that crowd was so drunk or so full of hate as to be blind to who they were facing. Every man in the porch in front of the jail was good with his guns. If the crowd forced things through there would be a terrible toll in lives before their aim could be achieved.

"Dusty!" the voice came to him from the office. "It's me, Gillem. I've brought my boys to help you out."

"Come ahead, Matt," Dusty replied.

The lynch mob stood watching as Matt Gillem and his three men came into view. It gave pause to the mob for each of the men held a ten-gauge shotgun and knew how to handle it.

"Rush 'em!" Fang screamed out. "Rush 'em. They won't shoot you. Go—."

A half-eaten apple flew across the street, thrown by the scar-faced Texas man as he and his men came into sight. Full into Fang's face the apple crashed and the gambler fell backwards from the hitching rail.

"That's a wicked waste of food, Stone," the handsome, red-hair young man at his right remarked, then put the petmakers to his horse.

The mob scattered as hooves thundered and they saw the Texans coming at them headed by the racing chuckwagon. Men tumbled over themselves to get back and to avoid being ridden down. The chuckwagon came to a halt, its driver substituting a worn eight-gauge muzzle-loading shotgun for the ribbons. Like trained cavalry the men riding alongside fanned out, bringing their horses round to face the crowd. The young man with the scarred face looked back at Dusty Fog. "You've got yourself a few deputies, Captain Fog."

"Yowee!" Rusty Willis whooped. "You come just in time, Stone."

The crowd held back, watchful and the rumblings of rage dying down. They knew, most of them, who the new arrivals were. The scarred faced young man was Stone Hart, leader of the Wedge, Rusty Willis and Doc Leroy's boss. Fanning out in a line between Stone Hart and his cook, Chow Willicka, in the wagon, were the other permanent members of the crew. Tall, lean, middle-aged Waggles Harrison, the foreman. Tall, red haired, handsome dandy Johnny Raybold, the scout of the outfit. Next was a short, stocky rider called Silent Churchman, known to belie both names. Seated a grulla, next to the wagon and looking miserable, was a medium-sized man with a long, drooping moustache. He was Peaceful Gunn, last but by no means least of the Wedge crew, as tough a bunch of riders as could be found anywhere in the West.

It was a bunch which would hold back any crowd, particularly when backed by three shotgun armed men. Still more when they were siding Dusty Fog, Mark Counter and the Ysabel Kid.

Dusty saw the wavering again and knew that he must strike while the iron was hot. The crowd were seeing that they could only take Happy Day by force and now the odds were even greater against doing it. Dusty was about to speak when Stone Hart asked, "What's it all about?"

"They're protecting one of them murdering Calhouns," Fang yelled back. He could see there was still a chance if he could persuade Stone Hart and his men to change sides. "We want him."

"Who says he's a Calhoun?" Stone inquired.

Some of the crowd were wondering the same thing now it was pointed out to them. "Yeah, Fang," a miner turned to look back at the gambler. "Who says that young feller's a Calhoun. I've met him and he's a real nice young feller. Besides he works for Miss Roxie."

This time the rumble of agreement was not the savage mob snarl, but more in a query. "Where's the feller who recognised him at, Fang?" another man shouted.

"Down to Bearcat Annie's," Fang replied, seeing a way out. The man would identify Happy Day and the mob would feel justified in taking the law into their own hands. The presence of the Wedge and the shotgun guards would add to the fury of the men, stir them into action. "I'll get him."

"Stay where you are," Dusty snapped. "Don't chance it Fang, or I'll cut you down. One of you men go fetch him."

The crowd quietened down, night was coming on now and the sun dropping down towards the horizon. There was still more than enough light for them to see what they were doing even yet. The crowd stood back waiting. Stone Hart swung down from his horse and went on to the porch, nodding to his two hands, then speaking to Dusty. "There's a one-eyed man in the game, Cap'n Fog," he said. "That *hombre* in the saloon doesn't seem to think they should be lynching this Calhoun."

"Neither do I," Dusty answered; he knew Stone Hart by reputation. Stone, like Dusty, was an ex-Confederate officer although they had never met. That scar was caused by a Union Army sabre, and the man who caused it never made another.

The eyes of the crowd were all on Bearcat Annie's saloon. They saw a man come from the side door with the miner who had gone to fetch him. The two men started to walk towards the crowd and from behind them a shadowy shape came to the side door of the saloon.

"Drop!" Dusty suddenly yelled, his right hand gun coming out, lining and firing in one flickering blurr of movement. The bullet hummed over the head of the buckskin-dressed man, splattering into the wall of the saloon near the door. At the same movement a shot roared from the shadowy shape but his aim was put off by Dusty's bullet. The shot ripped the hat from the man's head as he, with remarkable presence of mind, dropped to the ground.

Fang saw what was happening and knew he must get away. His hand dropped to his side. Across the street he saw the Ysabel Kid's lithe figure lunging forward, bowie knife sweeping up and then flickering out as he threw it. Fang's gun was almost clear of leather when he stiffened, something smashing into him. His hands clawed up in a convulsive move at the ivory hilt of the bowie knife which seemed to be sprouting from his chest. For a brief couple of seconds he stood there, then hunched forward and fell down.

The buckskin-dressed man was up and running, making for the jail as fast as he could go. He swung up on the porch but there was no more shooting from the saloon.

"You're the man who started all this," Dusty said to him. "Is Happy here one of the Calhoun gang?"

"I never said he was," the other man replied. "Sure his name's Calhoun. Mine's James, but that don't make me a kin to ole Dingus and Frank." His eyes went to the crowd, contempt and disgust lashing at them. "His name's Calhoun and he was with Bronco when he was a button, but he never rode with gang. You take off his shirt and see the scars Bronco left, whipping him, to make him ride with the gang. He never did."

"Reckon you'd best tell them all you know," Dusty remarked, watching the Kid swing from the porch and go through the crowd. Men older than the black-dressed boy, bigger and stronger also, made way for the Ysabel Kid as he went to collect his knife.

"Sure I'll tell 'em. It'll happen make them real proud. I met Happy Day in Sioux country. He was riding scout for the Army. It was him who got out of Fort Jo when the Sioux surrounded it. Snuck through the Sioux and stole one of their hosses to get away. Five of 'em followed him, we found them on the way back. One put an arrow into him but he kept on riding. You likely heard what happened. He got to Carrington and they relieved the fort. I went with them and took a bullet. I was in hospital, that's where I saw his back. He was unconscious and raving. I learned who he was then. Bronco Calhoun took him and his mother off a stage and made them stop with him. He tried to turn Happy there into one of his gang and Happy wouldn't. He killed Happy's mother."

The crowd were uneasy now, looking at each other. Happy Day felt a warm hand in his. Roxie was moving forward, her eyes blazing as she looked at the mob. "That's the sort of man you're going to lynch!"

One of the miners stepped forward, his face sheepish and his eyes on the ground. Then he braced back his shoulders and looked at Happy. "Ain't much a man can say, friend. But I reckon every man here's real ashamed and sorry for what's just happened."

"Not as sorry as you'd have been had you tried it," Dusty answered, then as the Kid joined him snapped. "Let's go."

"Where are you going, Dusty?" Roxie asked although she could guess the answer even before it was given.

"To Bearcat Annie's place. This time she's gone way too far."

A woman came around the side of the jail, running at a speed which belied her age. It was Matt Gillem's wife, her face ashy white at the strain. "Cap'n Fog," she gasped, and a man caught her, supporting her. "Cap'n Fog. It's the Calhoun gang!"

"Where, ma'am?" Dusty was from the porch.

"Headed for the bank, I saw them and came right off."

Then Dusty saw the reason for the lynching attempt. Saw it even as he started to give his orders. "Stone, your boys are deputised. Let's go."

The Texans left their horses, they would be better off fighting on foot. All the crowd gave angry yells and started to follow Dusty and his men; he did not try to stop them, knowing it would be no use and a waste of time to try.

Roxie suddenly realised Happy was not going with the other men. She looked at him, his face was working with emotion. Then he went to swing astride Johnny Raybold's big *bayo coyote* horse. The girl watched him, a sudden sick hurt coming over her.

Happy Day was not headed for the bank. He was riding out of town. Choking down the rising tears Roxie mounted Peaceful Gunn's roan. Disregarding the fact she was showing more of her legs than a young lady should, she rode after him. If Happy Day was deserting her and leaving town it meant he had fooled them all. He really was one of the gang. In that case she was going to kill him.

CHAPTER TWELVE

I'm Dayton, Remember Me?

Bronco Calhoun watched his men swinging from their horses in front of the Quiet Town bank. His sons and the four remaining men taken on since they came to town were to do the actual hold-up while he, as was his custom, stayed outside. From the town they heard the mob roar still rising. Calhoun nodded and his three sons led the way into the bank, guns in hand.

Standing with his shoulder rammed against the wall of a building Bronco Calhoun listened to the noise. He could tell there was a slightly different sound to it. Then it died away and a single shot came to his ears. He could not hear the shot fired in the saloon. Something told him all was not going according to plan, his instincts, worn fine by long years of dangerous trails, warned him. He was sure he had seen a woman come from a house nearby, Gillem's house, now he came to think about it. She had come out, glanced at him and walked away.

What worried him was he could not get over the feeling she had been watching him and his men. Bronco Calhoun was no fool. A man did not defy the law, even the rough and ready frontier law of the West, without a whole lot of savvy. One thing he never did was underestimate the thinking powers of others. The old woman might have recognised him, his face was on many wanted posters and his description circulated. She could have recognised him, or maybe guessed from the action of his men what was happening. Instead of panicking she left her house as if going for a stroll, came on to the street without any sign of suspicion. Right now she would, or could, be going for help.

The mob roar had died down now. He twisted to try and see what was happening in the bank. He could guess; the tellers would be lined up with hands raised and some of his men were scooping money into cornsacks. Soon they would be coming out and making for their horses for the rapid ride into the fast coming dark and safety.

It was then Bronco Calhoun heard a sound which made him swing round. His senses were as keen and alert as any animal's and the faint noise which attracted his attention would have gone unnoticed by many a man. He caught the sound and knew what it was; men were coming, several men. It took the old outlaw just half a second to decide what to do. He could stay and warn the other men, or he could make good his escape. His feet were already moving as he made his decision. Like the other men he had ridden to the bank and his horse was tethered with the others in front of the building. That was why the other men trusted him to stay outside and keep watch for them. What they did not know, not even his sons, was he had taken the precaution of leaving a second horse out back of town. The three sons who were left to him were not smart, he regarded them as he did the strangers working with him, as tools. There was no remorse in him as he turned to desert them. Even as he faded down an alley between two houses he saw the Texas men coming towards the bank.

Grat Calhoun led the other men from the bank, glancing around. What he saw made him drop his cornsack and claw at the gun in his holster. The rest of the gang came crowding out behind him and halted as they saw men moving in on them. It was then Kennet showed his courage. Like the tellers he had been held under by the guns of the gang, remembering Dusty Fog's advice and not trying anything. He had been forced to open the safe under threat of having his tellers killed, watched the money swept into cornsacks. Then the gang left and he heard angry curses, guessing something was wrong. He moved fast, crossing the floor and bringing the powerful door of the bank swinging closed behind the men. One of the gang saw the door moving. He tried to stop it but Kennet, with the strength of desperation, slammed it and jerked across one of the bolts.

Dusty Fog led his men forward, seeing the gang coming out of the bank. His hands crossed and brought the guns out. "Throw 'em high!" he shouted.

Grat Calhoun's gun came up, firing before he had lined it. Flame blossomed from Dusty Fog's gun barrels and the outlaw went backwards into the other men, throwing them into confusion. The rest of the gang elected to fight, guns coming out as the other men swarmed up behind Dusty Fog and from between other houses. Guns roared and crashed around the front of the bank, the outlaws breaking for their horses, shooting as they went. Two more of the men went down, one of Bronco Calhoun's sons and a fast shooting Texan who put down a miner and wounded another before he fell. The last Calhoun pitched over, hands clawing at the reins of his horse. Another man dropped the cornsack he was carrying, his gun swinging at the Ysabel Kid who was darting forward fast. The fast-moving young man dived over the hitching rail at the side of the street, landing and bringing his old Dragoon gun into line. Twice he fired and the man went down.

Then the remains of the Calhoun gang were on their horses, two men riding through a hail of lead, one bleeding badly. They got clear and raced out of town, but they went empty handed. The robbery of the Quiet Town bank, like the attempt at Northfield* many years after, came to nothing. A tough gang was shattered by the guns of the enraged and honest men of the town.

Dusty was the first man to the bodies, even as the wind blew gunsmoke from the street. He went carefully for with men like those one did not take chances. One gun was out and ready for use as he went forward. With his left hand he rolled Grat Calhoun over and looked down; the man was dead. That figured, Dusty did not have the time to attempt any fancy shooting. In an affair like that a man shot to kill and tried to make every shot count. He glanced around at the other men who crowded up and were examining the other bodies. Mark Counter went to each in turn, then came back to Dusty. "They've all cashed, but we didn't get Bronco."

"He's the one we wanted," Dusty answered.

"Hold it, Dusty!" The Kid moved forward. "I was near on sure I saw someone sneak off down between the houses. It'd be real like him to do that."

"Rusty, take charge here," Dusty snapped. "Mark, Lon, Doc, let's go."

There was no chance of getting Bronco Calhoun now, for the old outlaw would have hidden a horse somewhere

*Made by the James brothers and their gang

nearby and even now would be headed for it. He would be long gone before they got to where he had hidden it. One thing Dusty knew, he meant to have Bronco Calhoun this time. If he did not the Ysabel Kid would have lost his skill at following a track.

The Ysabel Kid was thinking the same thing. He took it as a personal slight that he missed connecting the man he had seen disappearing with Bronco Calhoun. Now he promised himself that he would take after the wily old outlaw and stick to the trail until one of them died.

Bronco Calhoun, not knowing he was the cause of the Ysabel Kid making such a grim decision moved between the houses and along the quiet streets of the town. He shambled along, ignoring the people who came from houses as guns roared. They were all talking, shouting to each other and pointing, not one of them gave him a second look. He looked like any other old drifter who might be ambling around the town. He felt relieved when he was through the houses, ahead was one of the deserted freight company buildings. Behind it, at the corral, was the horse he had taken and staked out before he even went back to collect his gang.

For a time he was thinking about the man the crowd were to have lynched. The man they said was a Calhoun. It was not one of his sons for they were all with him when the word went out. Then he remembered the woman he had taken from the stagecoach and the boy he had tried to turn into a vicious killer like the rest of the Calhoun clan. The hair on the back of old Bronco Calhoun's neck rose as he remembered Dayton Calhoun, looking at him after a whipping and saying, "One day I'm going to kill you."

The man at the jail could not be Dayton. The boy was dead. Left afoot, his mother dead and likely his head broke by the gun barrel, he could not be alive. The Sioux were out and the boy must be dead. If he was not—. Bronco Calhoun felt a cold hand on him. He remembered that boy very well, remembered thinking what a deadly fighting man young Dayton would be. There was something about that boy, even then, that Bronco could recognise. That deep capacity for hating which made a man a killer.

The corral was ahead now and he could see the horse standing where he had left it saddled and waiting for him. The horse snorted as he came nearer, his pace quickening and for once his usual wolf caution deserted him. The shooting ended behind him and he knew his absence would be noted by those Texan boys who ran the law. He did not know if he had been seen but it was not a good time for a man to wait round to find out. He was unfastening the reins when a voice from off to his right said: "Riding out, paw?"

Calhoun twisted round. A tall, buckskin-dressed young man came from where he had been standing concealed by the corner post of the corral. The young man shoved back his Union campaign hat with his left hand, the right never moving from where it hung by his gun butt. There was something in his eyes that made Bronco Calhoun pause and study the young man, reading more than just a friendly greeting in the words. Letting loose of the reins Calhoun turned to face the newcomer, an ingratiating grin coming to his face. It was the grin which had disarmed a young sheriff one time. Bronco Calhoun left the sheriff on the floor with a bullet through his stomach.

"Who be ye, son?" he inquired, knowing this was no chance meeting.

"I'm Dayton, remember me?"

Dayton. The word hit Calhoun like a club. He had almost been sure who this hate-faced young man was.

Now he knew for sure and for the first time in his life really felt scared.

"I mind ye, boy. But it's been some time since I saw you last. Sorry I can't spend time talking to you. I'm in a smidging of a hurry. You knows how it be with a man like me?"

"I know how it is," Happy answered. "I know real good. But you're not going any place. That'll be the boys getting shot, wouldn't it?"

"Don't know what you're talking about, boy." Calhoun lifted his left hand to the saddlehorn.

"You know all right. You've left your bunch at the bank. They'll be going under now. Or have gone under. You're the only one left."

"That's right, boy. I'm the only one left. So I'll be headed out afore they know I'm gone."

Happy looked at the man who had whipped the skin from his back more than once and his voice dripped hatred. "Like I said, you ain't going no place."

"You won't let them Johnny Rebs get me, will you, boy?" There was a whine in Bronco Calhoun's voice which was not entirely acting. He was afraid now, more than at any other time in his life. "They'd hang me for sure, boy. You can't let them do it to me, boy. Not to your own father."

"You're not my father. And they won't hang you."

"They sure will." Calhoun watched Happy's face, trying to locate some sign of mercy. All he could see was the bitter, cold hatred which had turned an amiable youngster into a merciless hunter, seeking out his prey. "You know what them Rebs are."

"Sure I do. Alvin Travis was one of them. He found me when you'd pulled out. He taught me everything I know." Happy's hand moved, the fingers crooked slightly, ready to lift the gun out. "Fill your hand."

For an instant Bronco Calhoun thought of accepting the challenge. Then he noted the stance, that relaxed yet so-ready way of standing. It told him that whatever Dayton might be he was a skilled man with a gun. He was in a class which the wily outlaw did not intend to match in a fair fight. "I'm not stacking out against you, boy. I'm an old man, wouldn't have no chance against you."

Slowly Calhoun lowered his left hand, keeping it well clear of his gun butt. He unbuckled the gunbelt and allowed it to fall to his feet. Happy watched, his hands working, the fingers moving slowly, not with nervous tension but with controlled and deadly rage. He knew and Bronco Calhoun knew, that he could not shoot down an unarmed man.

"My mother didn't have a chance against you. I'm going to kill you, old man. Just like I killed Deke."

"It was you killed Deke, was it?" Calhoun growled, for a moment his anger almost taking control of him. "Why'd you do it?"

"To stop him backshooting as square a man as ever walked. Mark Counter licked Bert fair enough. That's all you Calhouns were good for, backshooting."

Bronco Calhoun held down his anger. "You killed your half-brother," he hissed, watching for a chance to escape.

"I'd do it again. Those Texans played square with me. They gave me a chance to remember there were decent men alive. A man hunts lobo wolves all the time he gets to forget there's other animals. Dusty Fog, Mark Counter and the Ysabel Kid helped me remember that. I prayed you'd try and get Mark for killing Bert, but you didn't. You stayed back and let them handle the dirty work, just like you always did. Like today. I knew you'd pull out and leave the rest when the shooting started. So I got a hoss and come round the town looking for your hoss. Then I stayed here and waited."

Bronco Calhoun's face did not change expression. He knew there was no way out but to kill this young man. He meant to kill Happy anyway, such a dangerous young man would never leave his trail. While Happy was alive Bronco Calhoun would never know a peaceful moment again.

"You going to kill me, boy?"

"One way or another."

"Then let me pray first."

"You pray?" There was disbelief in Happy's voice.

"I led a bad life, son." The whine was in the voice again, an old man begging for a favour. "Let me make my peace."

Happy hesitated; he had heard of men repenting when death was close to them but did not believe it. He watched Bronco Calhoun remove his battered old black hat and hold it in front of his body, while his right hand slipped under it. Happy Day knew Bronco Calhoun well, very well. That was why he had circled the town and found the hidden horse, then waited. He knew Calhoun would try and escape, that was why he did not go with Dusty Fog and the others. Dusty was a fighting man, a very intelligent one at that. He did not know the way of Calhoun, the wily, savage old wolf. Happy did, he knew it very well.

For all his knowledge Happy was making a bad mistake. He was ignoring one of the rules Dusty had pressed on his deputies by allowing Bronco Calhoun to put a hand out of sight. It was a real bad mistake. There was one thing which Happy Day did not know about Bronco Calhoun. It was a thing which had cost other men their lives and was now likely to cost Happy Day his.

Inside the hat, fastened to the crown, was a Remington Double Derringer. It was a concealed weapon which never failed. Bronco Calhoun's hand curled around the butt as he piously raised his eyes to the sky. Happy relaxed for a vital instant.

Like a flash Bronco Calhoun brought the gun out from under his hat, thumb pulling back the hammer and firing. Happy rocked back on his heels, caught in the right shoulder by the .41 calibre bullet. He was knocked off balance his arm numb and helpless as he crashed into the corral wall.

"Smart boy, ain't you?" Calhoun sneered. "Real high minded and smart. I'm going to give you what I should have done that other time."

Desperately Happy tried to get his gun out with his left hand. Bronco Calhoun pulled back the hammer of the Derringer again, his sadistic mind preventing him from finishing Happy straight away. He lined the gun again and held it, finger tightening on the trigger.

The roar of a rifle came from the side of the corral opposite to where Happy had been standing. Bronco Calhoun spun round, his wild triggered shot going off into the air. Even as he fell Roxie Delue came running towards Happy, dropping the Sharps carbine she had taken from Peaceful Gunn's saddle-boot. "Happy, I couldn't let him kill you. I—I—." Happy patted her shoulder with his good hand, then he winced and she pushed herself back from him. She saw the wound and for the first time in her life Roxie Delue panicked. She had handled bullet and arrow wounds before but this one was different. Her hands shook and she gasped out, "Happy, you're hurt. Oh, Happy."

Soon after, even before the girl recovered herself, they heard footsteps and men came running up. Dusty Fog came to a halt, he looked down at the body on the ground. "Bronco Calhoun?" he asked.

"Sure." Happy gritted despite the pain from his shoulder.

"Doc, take care of Happy. How'd you all get here, Miss Roxie?"

Roxie explained, she saw other men approaching and recognised the Wedge cowhands. She suddenly realised she had stolen one of their horses and Happy another. The Texans would not be pleased with that.

Doc Leroy glanced at the wound then grunted. "I can't handle it here. Was we to have hosses I'd say take him to the jail and I'd handle it."

"Got two hosses here," Roxie answered. "We kinda borrowed them to come out and find Calhoun."

Dusty grinned. The girl was recovering her nerves again. She met Stone Hart's eyes without flinching and went to collect both the horses. Peaceful Gunn eyed his horse and groaned. "Went and lost me rifle."

"Naw," Roxie answered, knowing an apology was not needed. "I threwed the fool thing away. Whyn't you get a decent gun."

"A man of peace don't rightly need one, ma'am," Peaceful explained.

Doc helped Happy into the saddle then they rode back to the jail while the other men waited for Dusty's orders. "Stone, leave a couple of your boys here with the body. Mark, Lon, let's get back to the jail. We've got us some work to do."

Stone Hart watched Dusty; there was a hard glint in the small Texan's eyes. "What you figure's happening?" he asked. "There's more to this than meets the eye. Like you said, they've been hid around town, this bunch. Men can hide easy, hosses are harder. Man'd need a tolerable piece of room to hide a dozen or more hosses."

The two men had talked over the situation as they

came after Calhoun. Dusty was hearing only what he thought himself. He had known that the horses would take some hiding and had checked on the livery barns to find out if he could locate them. He failed and was still worried as to where Bronco Calhoun and his men hid out. Not one of the men of the gang left were alive to tell him and he could not allow time to take a posse out after the two who escaped. There was something far more urgent to be handled at that moment.

Arriving at the jail, Dusty snapped: "Load up, all of you. We've got a showdown with Bearcat Annie's bunch."

The men loaded their guns, all attention on the small Texan who was their leader. Dusty stripped the foil from combustible cartridges and loaded them into the chambers of his guns. The other men were all working, Maggie Bollinger, her husband, Dutchy and Eeney were watching the preparations. Roxie Delue came in with Doc Leroy. "Happy's going to be all right," the girl said, her cheeks flushed with happiness. "Where are you boys going?"

"Down the street a piece," Dusty replied.

"To Bearcat Annie's?"

"Yeah. I figger she's frayed her cinch rope. Time had to come when she got to be stopped. I figger the time's right now," Dusty answered.

The door of the jail opened and Derringer came in. "You going to the saloon, Cap'n Fog?" he asked.

"You reckon I wouldn't?"

"Nope, and neither does Bearcat Annie. She's waiting in there, only one door that ain't locked, the front one."

"And?" Dusty watched the gambler's face, knowing there was more than that to Derringer's quiet spoken words.

"She's got her near on twenty guns backing her up.

They'll cut you down as soon as you go in through the door."

None of the Texans spoke for a moment, then the Ysabel Kid asked, "Why'd you come to tell us that. You work for her?"

"I deal for her, same as you ride for the OD Connected. Difference being I don't owe her any loyalty. I'm fairly honest, and I know when to back a lawman. Cap'n Fog played square with me, I'm paying him back."

Gillem and the rest of the City Fathers crowded in, congratulating Dusty on breaking up the lynch mob and the gang. It was dark now and Dusty disregarded the men. He was standing by the window and looking along the street at the saloon. For a time he did not speak, making his plans. Then he turned to the other men, he could see people moving along the streets and knew the men in Bearcat Annie's place could not keep a very careful check on who came and went.

"Derringer, who's up in the rooms on the first floor?"

"All empty as far as I know. Use the middle room for big stake games but there aren't any tonight. The small side rooms are where Bearcat's girls do their entertaining."

"Then if we could get up on to the verandah and through the rooms we could get in without them knowing. Mark, Lon, we're going to give her a whirl."

"You got four deputies, Dusty," Doc Leroy remarked gently. "Don't recall us being fired."

Dusty looked at the two men and a grin split his face. "All right, five of us. Stone, you hold your boys to come in when you hear the Rebel yell, or shooting. You do that?"

"Rusty and Doc are part of my crew. They'll likely need help. I'll do it."

Maggie Bollinger went towards the door, then she

stopped and looked at Dusty. "I'm still one of your deputies, Cap'n. Reckon it's up to me to bring in Bearcat Annie."

"No!" Dusty snapped back. "They'll down you as soon as you go in that door."

"They won't shoot a woman, Cap'n. Reckon Bearcat'll need some taking. The guns'll be watching us."

Dusty knew what Maggie meant. He did not like it but could see from the set of her jaw that for once she was willing to go against his orders. It would create a diversion and might help. Derringer looked Maggie over, then warned, "She's got six or eight more gals in with her."

"Looks like you'll need help, Maggie," Roxie remarked. "Come on."

Eeney looked at her husband. "Hans, I made you a promise. I want your permission to break it."

Dutchy frowned. Eeney had promised that she would never again fight with another woman. It was in an attempt to stop her taking up Bearcat Annie's challenge that the promise had been made. Yet she knew that she must help Maggie and Roxie for the owner of the saloon would not surrender. Dutchy did not want Eeney involved, then he remembered the way Dusty Fog stood by him. He could not help in the taking of the saloon himself. Eeney not only could but would be of use. There was only one thing he could say.

"You have my permission."

Eeney felt herself trembling as she went to join the other two women at the door. One thing she promised herself was that she, not Maggie Bollinger, would be the one to settle accounts with Bearcat Annie.

CHAPTER THIRTEEN

Battle In Bearcat Annie's

Dusty Fog glanced at his deputies; Doc and Rusty each thrust a second revolver into their waistbands and the Kid took up his Winchester rifle. In an affair of this kind he preferred the extra magazine capacity of the long gun. The three women were looking at each other, Maggie Bollinger cool and detached, Roxie flushed and excited looking, while Eeney's face was pale and set. It was Maggie who spoke. She looked the other two over; they all wore low-heeled shoes and gingham dresses. It was for the second time of the day Roxie wished she was wearing her jeans and shirt waist for she knew there was going to be a fight. Bearcat Annie would never give up without one. "We're ready, Cap'n."

"Let's go," Dusty said calmly, then glanced at the women. "You ladies don't have to go through with this."

"Neither do you, Cap'n, but you're doing it," Maggie answered. "It'd be a poor woman as wouldn't fight for her home. That fat cow's the one behind all the trouble in this town. It's time we had a showdown."

"All right," Dusty smiled, watching the set and determined faces. "One thing, she's got her at least six gals backing her. Reckon you'll have to handle them, Maggie. You and Roxie, let Mrs. Schulze take Bearcat."

"Thought that myself," Maggie answered. "Come on, let's get started."

They all left the jail office by the back way. Roxie glanced at Happy who lay sleeping on one of the beds, his arm bandaged and held in a sling. She went over and kissed him lightly, then followed the others.

They moved along the back streets, past the high wall which surrounded the back of the saloon. There was no chance of effecting an entry from that side, the gate of the fence was locked and beyond it the saloon doors were all locked. Not a chance of breaking the locks quietly to allow them to get inside undetected. The only way was up over the verandah, through the rooms on the first floor, then down the stairs. It would be dangerous but with the diversion the girls meant to provide it was just possible.

Dusty gave a few words to his deputies as they moved along the alley between Bearcat Annie's place. "We're going to have to let the girls settle with Bearcat Annie before we make our move. It'll be a hell of a tangle and some of the guns might get hold of one of them to use as cover. Maggie, soon as you see us in place get out, all of you."

Maggie Bollinger laughed. "Just like that?"

"It will not be that easy, Captain," Eeney went on. "You may think women can't fight, you'll see different. We'll try to get clear, but there isn't much chance of it."

They were now by the wall on Grant Street, the verandah just above them. Mark held his sixty foot rope and looked up, seeing the first snag, there was no place where he could toss his noose around. "Hold it, Maggie," he said gently.

The three women stopped, Grant Street on this side was deserted now for the people of Quiet Town knew a showdown was coming between Bearcat Annie and the Texas lawmen. It would not be a safe location in front of the saloon when lead started to fly. Down at the jail Stone Hart, his men and the city fathers stood with their guns, ready for action when either they heard shooting or the Rebel yell.

Mark slung the rope over his shoulder again and glanced at the other men. Dusty was the lightest, but not tall enough to reach the balcony. It would have to be either the Kid or Doc. Mark glanced at the Kid, then turned with his back to the wall, cupping his hands, holding them out "Ready, Lon?" he asked.

"Ready." The Kid handed his rifle to Dusty and stepped forward. Putting his right foot into the cupped hand he shoved with the left as Mark's powerful muscles heaved. The Kid went up like he was rocket-propelled, Mark changed grips, his left hand holding the right foot, his right getting the Kid's other. Then he lifted, sweat pouring down his face as his giant frame took the strain. The Ysabel Kid felt himself lifting and his reaching hands caught the edge of the verandah. With a heave he pulled himself up and over the rail. His hand went across to bring his knife out as he stood looking around. Thrusting the point of his knife into the wood of the verandah he leaned over and caught the end of the rope Dusty tossed to him. Moving fast now the Kid secured the rope, then whistled softly. The rope jerked as Mark came up it hand over hand; the Kid helped his friend over the rail and Mark flattened against the wall near the window of one of the small side rooms. The window was open at the bottom and Mark waited for the others to come up before making an entrance. Dusty was the next up, then Doc. Rusty Willis fastened the Kid's rifle to the rope and went up himself then the Kid hauled his weapon up, looked over and waved to the three women.

"All right, girls," Maggie said. "Let's go."

Mark opened the window slowly, the Kid going in first. With almost catlike ability to see in the dark the Kid saw a bed. He also saw there was a lump which should not have been in an empty bed. Someone moved in the bed, rising slightly and turning up the small lamp which stood on a table beside the bed. A pretty young woman was sitting up, she did not appear to be wearing any clothes and pulled the sheets up, opening her mouth to scream.

The Ysabel Kid did not hesitate; he went forward like a leaping cougar. The girl was not alone in the bed. Even as the Kid landed on the bed he saw that. His hand closed over her mouth, stopping the scream before it was made. A man's clothes lay on the chair beside the bed and the Kid's knees drove into something which yielded under him. The girl arched her back, her eyes coldly menacing.

Watching the other men come in and make their way to the door the Kid relaxed his hand. The girl opened her mouth again but hard lips crushed down on it as the Kid kissed her. He relaxed and looked at the girl. "Look honeygirl, there's going to be bad trouble down there. Now I wants to grow old and ornery, not die young. So you just keep quiet. Make one sound and I'll come back and carve my name on your face."

The girl did not doubt the dangerous young man meant just what he said. She and her bedmate did not know what was happening in the saloon, they had been there most of the afternoon. She recognised the young men in the room, they were the town law. Bearcat Annie must have gone too far now and they were taking her. Beside her the man stirred but kept hidden by the sheets for he was a respectable business man of the town. He was one of the founders of the Civic Improvement Guild, also a married man with a wife who would not take kindly to his being there.

Dusty opened the door of the room and stepped on to the dimly lit balcony, the other men following him. Down below they heard women's voices. The Kid was the last man out; he turned at the door and winked at the girl. A scared man's face appeared and a voice usually booming and demanding, croaked, "What about me?"

"Figgered you was doing all right, friend. Do you a trade if you like." With that sentiment the Ysabel Kid closed the door behind him.

The gunmen in the saloon sat around; one was standing by a side window and watching the street. "Can't see anything happening yet," he called. "Jail's still quiet and there ain't anybody moving."

Bearcat Annie was not in the saloon but back in her office, the safe open and about to start destroying all the evidence against her. She knew the showdown was coming and also knew that sooner or later the law was going to get in. There were things in the safe which they must not find, for the rest she was satisfied that a good lawyer could get her off.

The six girls who stayed on had moved among the gunmen; there was little drinking being done and the place was cleaned up, bottles and glasses taken from the tables. There was not much noise; the girls were quiet and subdued and the men all alert.

They all saw the three women walk by the window and thought nothing of it until Maggie Bollinger shoved the batwings and came in. Roxie and Eeney followed her inside, moving one on each side of her. The dancehall girls looked in surprise for the women of the town never entered saloons. Bristling like alley cats the six painted girls moved together then came forward.

"Where's Bearcat Annie?" Maggie asked.

In her office Bearcat Annie heard the voice and went to the door. She saw the three townswomen and knew why they had come. She stepped out, eyes going to Eeney first, then Maggie and Roxie. So the women aimed to take her, not Dusty Fog. She did not mind, it would give her a chance to get her revenge on that German girl. "I'm here," she answered and stepped forward.

In her eagerness to tangle with Eeney, Bearcat Annie forgot to lock the safe or her office door. She went across the room and halted in front of Eeney, then looked at Maggie Bollinger. None of them spoke for an instant. They looked like cats as they waited for something to happen. Behind them the gunmen pushed back their chairs and moved under the balcony to give the women plenty of room. The man at the window, seeing himself cut off and knowing it would be unsafe to be there moved round to his friends.

"I'm arresting you," Maggie said, eyes on the big blonde.

"You are, are you?" Bearcat Annie spit the words out. "Why you fat cow, I'll teach you to come in here. Throw 'em out, girls!"

Roxie Delue swung a hard little fist as a red headed dancehall girl lunged at her, feeling it smash into the girl's nose. Then Roxie felt as if the top of her head was being torn off as another girl lunged in. The centre of the room was a mass of screaming, fighting women.

Eeney and Bearcat Annie hurled at each other. Eeney's fists were clenched and stabbed out hard but Bearcat Annie was impervious to pain. Her clawing hands dug deep into Eeney's hair and tore at it. A scream of pain tore from Eeney's lips, she forgot her fist-fighting training. Taking a double handful of the other woman's piled up blonde hair she drove her fingers in until they scratched Bearcat Annie's scalp, then pulled. Round they swung, clear of the others and staggered to one side screaming in rage.

The gunmen yelled their delight and approval, watching the fight which was to become a classic of the old West. The battle in Bearcat Annie's saloon was to be a legend and talked of the length and breadth of the West, from Texas to California. Miners, cowhands, soldiers and every other denizen of the open range would tell of it.

Roxie and Maggie were swamped over by screaming, clawing, kicking girls. One thing saved them. In the wild mêlée there was no chance of sorting out who was who. It became a case of tearing the nearest hair, kicking, punching, clawing or slapping wildly around, striking the nearest person. Roxie felt her frock rip as she tore the skirt from a screaming girl. It was a wild tangle of flailing arms and legs, screaming mouths, interspersed with ripping noises as clothes were torn. Then Maggie was on her feet, swinging round with a couple of clawing girls hanging to her. Her dress went, ripped off as the girls staggered back. She swung a wild blow which knocked a third girl backwards into the bar. The girl smashed into the polished wood and stood for an instant, her eyes glazed, then she stumbled forward into the wild tangle once more.

Bearcat Annie and Eeney reeled across the room, smashing into the bar and staggering off again. They stopped tearing at hair and swung wild slaps and punches which rocked each other. Bearcat's clawing hands gripped the neck of Eeney's frock and ripped at it, swinging Eeney and as the gingham tore sent her on to a table.

The big blonde hurled after Eeney, landing on top of her but the table's legs gave way and dumped them on the ground once more where they rolled and thrashed in a wild tangle of flailing arms and waving legs. Across the floor they rolled, first one, then the other getting on top. They hit the bandstand and still clinging to each other's hair got first to their knees, then to their feet. Eeney tried to push the other girl backwards; they hit the bandstand and Bearcat Annie was thrust on to it. She fell backwards and brought Eeney down with her. Eeney pushed the blonde backwards, and Annie landed on a stool, breaking the guitar which lay on it. She braced herself and lunged forward, her lowered head ramming into Eeney. Back they went, crashing into the piano. Eeney's fingers closed on Annie's head, dragging it down; they strained against each other, gasping and squealing. The piano started to move backwards as their weight came down on it. Smashing the flimsy rail around the side of the bandstand the piano went over, crashing to the floor with a hideous discordant jangle of the keys. Eeney and Bearcat Annie went with the piano; they crashed on to it and rolled over it, landing on the floor again. It was a brutal, savage fight with no holds barred. Bearcat Annie was well versed in this style of fighting; in her life she had been compelled to defend herself in other fights like this. Their frocks were gone by the time they got to their feet; both were naked to the waist but neither took any notice of it.

Coming to their feet again they staggered apart, gasping for breath. For an instant they stood like that, then hurled at each other once more. Eency struck out with wild fists now, feeling them strike home, then Annie lashed out back. Their fists landed home hard; Annie felt blood running from her nose, her right eye puffing up, Eeney, blood trickling from the corner of her mouth, her left eye starting to discolour, closed again, hands clawing out. Round and round they swung, lost their balance and hit the floor once more.

Up on the balcony Dusty Fog led his men forward and down the stairs. They held their guns but the gunmen did not see them. Every one of these gunmen was completely absorbed in watching the sight of the battling women; they could pay no attention to anything else. Dusty wondered if he could take the men but there was the danger that the fighting women might get in his way. He must wait until there was no danger. By his side Mark Counter watched Eeney and Bearcat Annie as they rolled over and fought; he had to hold himself from shouting to Eeney to use her fist-fighting skill instead of trying to match the big blonde in her own style of brawling.

The wild tangle of women broke up. Roxie clung to and locked one arm around the neck of a woman. She rolled right over the other woman and fought with her, not realising it was Maggie Bollinger she was tangling with. It was Maggie who recovered first. She yelled at Roxie and the wild light died in the girl's eyes. They got to their feet; other women were still fighting with each other. Maggie went forward, scooped up a pair of them and crashed their heads together, dropping them again. They lay limp and then the other women were up and the wild tangle joined once more. Roxie rocked under the impact of a wild, fist-swinging attack, her own fists lashing back.

Maggie staggered into the bar, a girl rushing at her. She ducked and caught the girl by the legs, heaving and straightening. The girl went over the bar out of sight and Maggie hurled herself at the three remaining girls who were ganging up on Roxie.

Bearcat Annie and Eeney fought their way back to

the bar. Annie locked her arms round the other woman's bare waist, squeezing hard. Eeney gasped in pain as she was crushed, her fists pounding at the blonde's face. There was enough steam behind the blows to make Bearcat Annie scream and tighten her hold. Then Eeney dug her fingers deep into the tangle of blonde hair and pulled with all her strength.

Annie howled like a train going into a tunnel. She swung Eeney round and lifted, throwing her on to the bar top. Eeney's feet came up into the blonde's face and pushed her hard, then Eeney fell over the bar and landed on the dancehall girl. The girl pushed Eeney over and got to her feet to attack her. It was a mistake. Bearcat Annie caught up a chair and seeing a head come up ran back and brought it smashing down. The girl gave a cry and went down again, Eeney forced herself up; the big blonde was leaning on the bar, gasping in pain and exhaustion. Eeney caught the woman's hair, jerked her head up and slammed it down on to the bar. Annie was dazed by the blow but her own hands laced into Eeney's tangled hair. She braced her foot against the bar and pulled. Eeney was forced to go over the bar, she felt as if the very scalp was being torn from her head. She was dragged over and on to the floor, hooking her leg behind Bearcat Annie's and bringing her down.

It was even worse now, Bearcat Annie fought with savage rage, her weight counting against Eeney. She threw a leg over the German girl, holding her down by sheer weight, then her hands gripped Eeney's hair and tried to smash the head on to the floor. Eeney braced her neck muscles trying to hold back the shattering force of the blows, but her head hit the floor hard. Her head was spinning and she could hardly keep up her strength to try and fight back, her hands weakly pushed at the heavy weight on her.

At the bar the rest of the women were all but spent; only two dancehall girls were left on their feet, struggling weakly with Roxie and Maggie. The big woman was just about ready to collapse, so were the others. Then Maggie saw her chance, she gripped Roxie by the hair with one hand, the other digging fingers into the back of one of the girls' neck. Then with all her strength she smashed the two skulls together, with the third girl's head between them. The girl moaned and went down in a limp heap, once more Maggie crashed the heads together and let Roxie and the last girl drop. She swayed herself and almost fell.

Bearcat Annie, still kneeling astride Eeney and trying to smash the other woman's head to the floor, looked up. She saw Maggie was the last woman on her feet and knew she must try and finish the black-haired woman off. She knotted her left hand in Feeny's hair and smashed a brutal right to her face, let her head flop back to the floor. Gripping the edge of a nearby table, the blonde tried to pull herself up. The table tipped over and Bearcat Annie dragged herself up by the edge. She swayed on her feet, sobbing in exhaustion as she started for Maggie Bollinger who stood with her legs braced apart and mouth hanging open.

Maggie was exhausted. She had taken the brunt of the attack by the saloon girls and was only barely conscious of what was happening. She saw the big saloon keeper standing but her mind would not focus or give her aching body any instructions. Bearcat Annie stumbled forward then as she came into range swung a wild haymaker. It smashed like a club into the other woman's cheek. Maggie's head rocked to one side, snapping over hard. She reeled back, smashing into the bar. Her legs gave way and allowed her to slide down until she sat on the floor with her back against the bar. Bearcat Annie looked down, swaying and almost falling, she gripped the bar to hold herself up and lifted her foot to stamp down on Maggie.

Laying on the floor Eeney felt pain welling over her; from head to foot she seemed to be a mass of bruises and pain. Then she sat up, dazedly, seeing Bearcat Annie staggering at Maggie. Weakly she reached out then gripped the edge of the table to drag herself up on to her knees. Her bruised bloody face showed her exhaustion, her eyes glassy. Through the swirling mists which whirled around her as she tried to get up she saw something. Hanging to the table Eeney's eyes managed to focus on the stairs, at Mark Counter. The big Texan had holstered his guns and was watching her, he saw her eyes meet his and clenching his fist swung it as if punching. Eeney gave a gasp, she recognised Mark even though her mind was so dazed that it would hardly function. Then she realised, this was the man who had helped her beat Russian Olga, telling her how to handle the other woman. She saw him make the punching motion once more and in a flash it came to her what he meant. She had fought Bearcat Annie under the big blonde woman's own terms instead of using the skill she had gained while travelling with Mundy's troupe. That was why she got whipped. Bearcat Annie knew more about all-in rough-house fighting than Eeney did.

It took all Eeney's will-power to shove herself to her feet, she could barely stand. The watching gunmen yelled with delight, they had thought the fight was over, now it looked as if the girl was going to carry on. They admired Eeney for her sheer guts and yelled the encouragement to her. Eeney was oblivious to it all and in her head there seemed to be a roaring. Yet she kept her feet and closed with Bearcat Annie who hung on to the bar and stamped weakly at Maggie, missing the first time. Eeney caught Bearcat Annie's bare shoulder and turned the other woman round, then swung her fist. She tried to keep up her fists in the way she had learned from Mundy, swinging again, rocking the big blonde's head back. Bearcat Annie felt the punch, it slammed into her mouth. With a moaning scream Bearcat Annie lunged forward but Eeney backed off, swinging a left then a right which rocked Bearcat Annie's head again.

Still holding her fists clenched Eeney followed the staggering blonde, at every step slamming another punch into the bloody face. Bearcat Annie was helpless now. Her hands flopping limp and helpless at her sides as the punches rocked her head from side to side and staggered her back across the room. Eeney shot out a right, her arm driving the fist full into Bearcat Annie's mouth. The big woman looked as if she was running backwards and hit the batwing doors, they parted just enough to allow her to go half out. Then she hung there, her arms over the top of the doors, holding her up.

Eeney almost fell; she clung to a table to help keep her feet. Behind her the gunmen crowded forward eager to see the end of the fight. Yet Eeney did not hear them. Sobbing in pain and exhaustion she staggered forward. There was only one thing she could see, Bearcat Annie's face, blood running from nose and mouth, one eye blackened, the other swelling and discoloured. Bearcat Annie hung there, helpless, mouth hanging open. She did not even know Eeney was coming nearer. The German woman halted, her breasts heaving and her fist clenching. She ached in every inch of her body, the agony of her hair, which felt as if the roots were on fire, the raw taste of blood in her throat, they were going now, sinking into numbness. With every ounce of her weight behind her she swung her fist. It was a beautiful punch, thrown with swing and power behind it. Bearcat Annie's head rocked, the batwing doors swung open and the big blonde went backwards. Her feet shot from under her and she fell on to her back in the street. Eeney staggered after her, out of the doors. Her legs were buckling as she crossed the sidewalk, down to the street and dropped forward, sinking on to her knees, astride the unconscious Bearcat Annie. Eeney's hands supported her for a moment, then as men and women came running towards her everything went black.

CHAPTER FOURTEEN

Rusty Willis Kills A Man

Dusty Fog and his deputies watched the fight in silence, only regretting they could not give their vocal encouragement to their three friends. The gunmen were completely absorbed in watching and not one of them made any attempt to turn around. Then as Eeney started to knock the battered Bearcat Annie across the floor Dusty tensed and nodded to his men. The other four were ready, they could see the time was fast coming for them to take a hand. Bearcat Annie and Eeney went through the door and with a shattering rebel yell Dusty Fog leapt from the stairs on to the floor, Mark Counter following him. The Ysabel Kid put a hand on the banister, vaulted over and landed catlike behind the gunmen, his rifle held hip high but ready to use.

The gunmen came round, hands hanging down towards guns, then freezing as they saw the five young men behind them. It was like Dusty had told Kennet, a good man with a gun knew just when to move and when he must stand immobile. It was time to stand right now. The hired guns knew who they were up against and knew that although they outnumbered the Texans they were still beaten.

"All right, throw them high!" Dusty snapped.

Any thought of hostile action was ended definitely by the arrival of Stone Hart and the other Wedge crew, entering the saloon with guns held ready. Dusty nodded his approval and thanks to Stone Hart, then glanced at the gunmen. There was no rancour in his look, these were just hired men and of no importance to him one way or the other.

Stone Hart looked around at the groaning, half-naked women and the wreck caused by the fight. "Man, looks like there's been a fair round in here," he said. "How about these bunch, Dusty?"

"Take them to wherever their hosses are and see they leave town," Dusty replied. "Handle it for me, will you, Stone! Mark, go fetch Mrs. Schulze and Bearcat Annie in here. Rusty, you make a round of the town, see all's quiet, then go back to the jail. Mark, Lon, we'll have a look in the office, see what's in the safe if we can open it."

Doc Leroy was busy examining the girls even as the hired guns were herded out under the experienced eyes of the Wedge crew. Dutchy, Cy Bollinger and Happy came in. The blacksmith was carrying Eeney and gently laid her on top of the bar. Then he turned and went to his wife, bending over her. Happy was by Roxie's side, his face showing anxiety. "Doc!" he gasped. "Come over here and look at Roxie."

"Already have, boy," Doc answered. "She's all right."

Men were crowding into the saloon now, all ogling

the half-naked and battered contestants. They were forced apart as Mark came through carrying the unconscious Bearcat Annie in his arms. He laid her on the floor and glanced around with some distaste. "All right," he barked. "Let's have this place cleared. Right now."

The crowd faded away. They had learned the way of the Texas boys by that time.

The saloon doors opened again and Mrs. Gillem came in with several other women behind her. The old woman glanced around, picked up Maggie Bollinger's torn gingham dress and grunted. "Looks like it was a real battle."

"Sure was, ma'am," Mark agreed. "Say, I lost my suggan, there's enough material here to make me a dandy one."

"I'll see about it," Mrs. Gillem promised.

That was how Mark Counter came to own a suggan, a kind of heavy patchwork quilt comfort made from, among other things, the clothing of the participants of the battle in Bearcat Annie's saloon.

"Reckon we can leave the ladies to handle things, with Doc's help," Dusty remarked. "Let's take a look in the office."

"Man, this is lucky," the Ysabel Kid remarked as they entered the office and found the safe door open. "Saves us trying to find a key."

The three Texans went to the safe and took out the papers. Dusty was about to check through them when he saw the bottle Bearcat Annie's husband had left. He pulled the cork out and a sweet, sickly aroma permeated the air. It was not the sort of thing one would expect to find in Bearcat Annie's safe although for a moment Dusty did not connect what it was with anything.

The Ysabel Kid's nostrils quivered, his keen senses working hard to try and locate where he had smelled that scent before. Then he remembered. "Remember that bunch who tried to stick Dutchy up?" he asked. "They smelled like they'd been round some of this stuff."

"And that Mexican we caught out at Dutchy's place," Dusty answered. "I've seen this stuff before but I can't place where."

Mark was leafing through the papers, he looked at the other two. "Reckon you called it wrong for once, Dusty. I make it Bearcat Annie was the big wheel."

Dusty glanced at the papers; there were title deeds to saloons, gambling houses, even some of the freight companies which had been driven out of business. The one thing there was not was money. The safe held nothing but papers, not a single dollar of cash.

"I'd sure like to know where she hid Calhoun's men out in town," Dusty remarked. "The men would be easy, but not the horses. We checked the livery barns and every one of the empty freight companies' buildings."

Mark picked a sheet of paper up from the bottom of the safe and blew dust from it, looking down at the faded print, then passing it to Dusty. "Reckon I could make a fair guess at where they were kept."

Dusty accepted the paper, glanced at it and nodded. Of course, that was the obvious answer. The one place other than either livery barn, freight company or stage-line which would have a fair number of horses around. The one place Dusty had never thought of looking in. He could see everything clearly now, it all added up to one thing. His guess was correct, Bearcat Annie was not the big wheel. That was when he remembered what the scent in the bottle was used for.

Rusty Willis walked the streets of Quiet Town and pondered on the way the townsfolk greeted him. When he came to town with the Wedge he was regarded either

as a wild heller on a spree or as a source of profit. Here
he was a respected and respectable member of the town
law. Even mothers with young daughters smiled at him
now.

He was on one of the quiet, semi-residential streets,
walking along at an easy pace, noting that the people
who lived there appeared to be at home instead of out
seeing the sights of the town. He was approaching a
building when he saw a buggy standing in front of him,
the horse facing in his direction. The buggy was in the
light of the windows and open door, an innocent enough
looking thing in a town like this. Rusty glanced at it and
gave it little thought. He got his bearings and saw the
the building was Buzzard Grimwood's establishment.
The two storey house and shop, the high plank fence
which surrounded his property, hiding from view his
large stables where he kept the teams for his hearses and
the hearses themselves.

A man came from the building, a slim man wearing
the dress of a professional gambler, grey cutaway coat
and white, low crowned hat showing plainly in the light.
Somehow he looked familiar to Rusty although the young
man could not tie him down.

Even as Rusty stood looking the man swung a carpetbag onto the seat of the buggy and came around to
get in. There was nothing wrong with the sight except
that Rusty was a lawman now and thought differently
from when he first rode into Quiet Town. The man might
be quite harmless and innocently visiting Grimwood. It
would do no harm to check up. Rusty was about to walk
forward when he remembered two of Dusty's instructions. Never approach a buggy in such a way the man
in it could run you down. Never, no matter how innocent
he looked, approach a suspect without being ready to
take action against him.

Quickly Rusty crossed the street, coming alongside

the man, hand hanging by the butt of his gun as he called, "Hold it up there, mister. I'm a deputy——."

The man in the buggy twisted around fast, seeing the badge glinting on Rusty Willis's vest. With a snarl the man sent his hand under his coat. The move was fast, very fast. Rusty could not equal such speed, but thanks to Dusty's warning he was not taken by surprise. Even as the short barrelled gun came from under the man's coat and roared Rusty was dropping. The bullet cut a hole in his hat brim as he landed on the ground, hand fanning to the butt of his old Dance gun. The heavy Confederate revolver came up, lining and roaring loud in Rusty's hand. For a copy of a Colt Dragoon the Dance made a fair job of shooting. The heavy ball caught the man in his chest, knocking him backwards from the buggy. The horse lunged forward, swinging the buggy into the sidewalk, one wheel catching a hitching post and slamming the vehicle to a halt. The carpetbag was thrown from the buggy; it burst open as it landed and in the light of the shop window Rusty saw money spill out.

Walking forward, his Dance gun held ready Rusty went to the man he had killed. People were coming from their houses, running towards him as he turned the body over and looked down at the face. Rusty straightened up, his face working as he recognised the man he had shot. Ignoring the crowd he holstered his gun, shoved the money back into the carpetbag and turned to make for the Bearcat Annie saloon to report to his boss. He wondered what Dusty was going to say.

Dusty Fog was coming from the office, followed by Mark Counter and the Ysabel Kid. They looked around. The place was empty now, the women upstairs in beds, dancehall girls and town women laying side by side recovering from the fight. The three Texans were going to collect the last and most vital member of the gang which brought terror and trouble to Quiet Town. They halted as Rusty came in, face lined with worry at what he had done.

"What's wrong, boy?" Dusty asked, glancing at the carpetbag Rusty held.

"I've just made a bad mistake, killed a man. Honest Dusty, I didn't recognise him, he wasn't wearing his usual clothes. When I spoke to him, told him I was a deputy, he drew and shot at me and I killed him."

"So?" Dusty asked, knowing there was more to it than that. Rusty would not be worried unless it was something real bad. Killing a man who acted like that was to be regretted, but necessary.

"It was Buzzard Grimwood. I didn't recognise him in that get-up and I killed him, Dusty."

Dusty glanced at the sheet of paper he held. The marriage certificate between Annie Gill and James Thornlay Grimwood. Then he looked at Rusty Willis and answered, "Good, you likely saved me having to do it."

THE END